Too Hot

Marie Tuhart

https://www.marietuhart.com/

QUALITY CONTROL: We strive to produce error-free books, but even with all the eyes that see the story during the production process, slips get by. So please, if you find a typo or any formatting issues, please let us know at marie@marietuhart.com so that we may correct it.

Thank you!

Too Hot

Wicked Sanctuary: Surrender your inhibitions.

A man who fights fires.

A woman terrified of open flames.

An attraction that blazes past barriers.

In the flickering shadows of Wicked Sanctuary, a story of opposites unfolds. Elementary school teacher, Brianna Copeland yearns for something more in her quiet life. After a conversation with a friend, she embarks on an unexpected journey.

Rafe Lyons, a hunky firefighter with a passion for fighting fire is surprised when Max pairs him with Brianna. This thrusts them into a dance of desire and discovery. Rafe is determined to help her get past her fear.

In the glow of Wicked Sanctuary's seductive flame, can they find love in the midst of their burning desires? One that promises to be as scorching as it is unforgettable.

ACKNOWLEGMENTS

Laurie, thank you for all your support and beta reading.

Red Quill Editing team, you are the best team to work with. You make me think, laugh, and as always, make me a better writer.

Publisher's Note: This book contains a dominant male, spunky heroine, sexy situations, fire play and arson. No Artificial Intelligence was used in the writing of this book.

To My Readers:

This book contains elements of the BDSM lifestyle that are only true in this book. There are various relationship dynamics in the lifestyle, which are decided between the people involved. While I have researched and talked with people in the lifestyle, this is my take on how my characters choose to live.

If you decide to explore the lifestyle yourself, please remember to always be safe. Never go home with someone you don't know. Attend a munch or a smaller get-together first to see if this is something you want in your life. Reading and living are very different.

Enjoy.

Chapter 1

Brianna Copeland clapped her hands to get her students' attention. "All right, everyone. Our special guests will be here shortly, so put away your books, and take your places at your tables."

Her second-grade students scrambled up from the floor where they'd been reading and put their books away in the bins in the back of the classroom. Slowly, they took their seats at their tables. She smiled at them before glancing out the window.

A police car had pulled up a moment ago, and now a fire truck joined the cruiser. Her students were so excited to hear from a real police officer and firefighter today. There was one fire truck, but three firefighters exited. Her gaze was captured by the one who climbed out of the back.

Oh my goodness. His dark blue shirt stretched over broad shoulders and was tucked into blue slacks. Her gaze continued down until she came to a pair of black boots. Heat filled her body. She forced her gaze away from his feet in time to see muscular arms flex as he shut the fire truck door.

He turned his head, and Brianna started to look away so he wouldn't catch her watching. But she noticed he was calling out to the police officer who'd exited his vehicle. What were their names? Oh, yeah, Officer Wolfe and Firefighters Lyons, Michaels, and Peters. It was

Lyons who held her attention, having met the other two firefighters before.

Wolfe and Lyons. What a combination. Two predators in the wild. She continued to watch as he shook hands with Officer Wolfe. For a moment, she let her mind wonder how it would feel to have those masculine hands on her body?

Brianna shook her head. What was wrong with her? She wasn't one to ogle men. That didn't stop her from watching until the two men disappeared from her sight.

"Miss Brianna," one of her students called.

She turned away from the window to see all her students at their tables. "Yes, Penny."

"How long before the firemen and policeman get here?" Penny wiggled in her seat.

"Shortly." She moved away from the window and smiled at her students. "Remember, while the terms Penny used are correct, there are women in those professions also. If possible, use firefighter and police officer."

"Yes, Miss Brianna," the kids chorused.

"I'm going to be a firefighter," Winter said.

"Me, I'm going to be a cop," Cooper commented.

"You can be anything you want," Brianna said.

More voices joined in on what they wanted to be when they grew up, and Brianna shook her head. They'd change their minds over the course of their lives, just as she had. Movement at the classroom door had her shifting.

"I believe they're here," she said as the door opened to reveal the principal.

* * * *

"Hey, Rafe."

Rafe Lyons turned. "Logan." He walked over and held out his hand. "How are you doing? Feeling better?" Logan had been shot several months ago. Luckily, it had been a leg wound. Serious, but not fatal.

"Right as rain. Having Ellie as a nursemaid did great things. I see your captain roped you into presenting at the school."

"Yeah, probably because I do double duty." The Pleasant Valley Fire Department wasn't big enough to require a full-time arson investigator, so he was a firefighter first, then an investigator.

"I get that. My boss offered to have others from the department come, but since it's second graders, he wanted to keep it basic."

Rafe laughed. "Basic? After what you went through in the last few months, I wouldn't call that basic." They walked toward the entrance. Out of the corner of his eye, Rafe saw a young woman standing at a window. Probably the teacher, but she looked too young. He sighed. He was only thirty-five but felt older than that.

"I heard about the fire over on twentieth street. Anyone hurt?" Logan asked.

"No." Rafe ran his hand through his hair. "It's the third fire in a week."

"Arson?"

"Not sure. There are no obvious clues." At the entrance, Rafe pushed the button, and within a minute, an older woman rushed to the door and pushed it open. "Welcome, gentleman. I'm Principal Meyers."

"Principal Meyers." Rafe inclined his head and held the door open for Logan. The other two firefighters stayed with the truck to prepare for the kids. He disliked how schools had to be so locked up to keep the kids safe.

Kids should be free to play. But that was the world they lived in.

Pleasant Valley wasn't a hot bed of shootings or anything that would threaten the kids, yet he was glad they were taking precautions.

"Ms. Copeland's classroom is this way. The children are excited." She bustled her way down the hall with him and Logan following.

When she stopped in front of a door, Rafe grinned. The door had been decorated for them. Fire trucks, police cars, badges, ladders, hoses, and handcuffs. Kids this age had big imaginations. He reached for the knob and held the door open for the principal.

The chattering of children reached his ears. A sharp jolt hit his heart. Would he ever have kids? Well, he'd have to find the right woman first, and there weren't any around who interested him at the moment.

The room went silent as the principal walked in. Logan followed, and Rafe closed the door behind him as the last to enter.

"Officer Wolfe and Firefighter Lyons, this is Brianna Copeland, the teacher," Principal Meyers said as she introduced them.

"Welcome, gentlemen." The woman he'd seen at the window stepped forward with her hand outstretched.

Rafe's gaze met hers as he took her hand in his. If he hadn't been looking at her, he would have missed the slight darkening of those hazel eyes as their skin met. He didn't want to release her hand. Logan cleared his throat. Rafe released his hold, and Brianna shook Logan's hand.

"We're so glad you're here today." Her voice was soft and soothing. This was the type of voice Rafe could see himself coming home to at night.

Whoa. He didn't even know anything about Brianna. His libido disagreed, but Rafe reined himself in. There was time to learn about this intriguing school teacher.

"I'll head back to my office now that you're in good hands." The principal left the room.

Rafe rubbed his palms on his thighs. *Oh yes, she was in good hands with him.* He shook the thought out of his mind. He was in a classroom full of kids.

"Would you like to stand or sit?" Brianna asked.

He kept his gaze on her flushed face. "I think standing will be fine."

"Yes." Logan nudged him in the side.

"Okay." She turned away.

"What's going on?" Logan whispered.

"Nothing." Rafe shook his head. A bomb of attraction hit him the second her hand touched his. Unusual for him, but for the first time in a long time, he wanted to pursue it.

"Well, keep it under wraps. We are in an elementary classroom."

Logan was right to remind him. He looked out at all the eager faces. He counted quickly. Twelve kids. A good class size.

"All right," Brianna said to the class. "Please remember your manners. Raise your hand to ask a question and wait to be called on." She gestured to him and Logan. "The floor is yours." She moved to the back of the room and sat at one of the empty tables, in the child size chair. She was a tiny thing, but it still surprised him that she fit.

"Hello, kids, I'm Officer Wolfe."

"And I'm Firefighter Lyons."

One of the little girls burst out laughing. "You're

named after animals."

The class laughed, and he and Logan both chuckled.

"One might think that. So how about, for today, you call us Rafe and Logan."

The kids turned to look at their teacher, and she nodded.

"Who has a question?" Logan asked. Twelve hands shot up, and off they went.

* * * *

Brianna sat at the table, trying not to ogle the firefighter. Rafe. That was his name. She hadn't met Logan until today but knew of him since she was friends with Ellie, his girlfriend.

She listened as the men answered the kids' questions. They were both patient and understanding. Brianna loved that about them, but especially how Rafe would get level with the kids, looking them in the eye as he spoke.

"Miss Brianna, can we go out and look at the fire truck, please?" Cooper asked.

She glanced at the two men leaning against her desk.

"We don't mind," Logan said.

It was only eleven, and lunch wasn't until twelve. "Okay."

The kids cheered. "Line up and no running." The kids jumped up and made a line starting at the door.

"Impressive," Rafe said when she grabbed her keys off the desk. "Boys usually have trouble following orders."

"You just have to know how to handle them." Brianna almost clamped her hand over her mouth. That came out all wrong. Rafe grinned. She shook her head and opened her classroom door. Waiting until the children filed out with Rafe and Logan behind them, she closed the door, then followed them outside.

Brianna was proud of her kids. They walked calmly and quietly outside and waited until Logan and Rafe led them to the vehicles. She hung back, allowing the kids to enjoy themselves.

Almost an hour later, the kids were out of questions and had been all over both vehicles. A bell went off.

"Lunch time," Penny yelled.

"What do you tell Officer Wolfe and Firefighter Lyons?" Brianna asked.

"Thank you." Twelve pairs of eyes turned to her. "Go. The principal will let you back into the school."

The kids ran for the door.

"I believe you're friends with Ellie, my girlfriend," Logan said as they watched the school door open, and the kids went inside.

"Yes. It's good to finally meet you." Brianna had met Ellie two months ago when she set up a birthday party for one of the other teachers, and they became friends. "Is your leg all healed up now?"

"It is. Is there anybody in this town who doesn't know I got shot?"

Rafe clapped Logan on the shoulder. "No."

There was friendship there. "Ellie told me about it. I had read in the newspaper about the shooting, but no names were mentioned."

"I'm glad she talked about it." Logan's radio went off. "Excuse me."

She was alone with Rafe. Brianna's tummy flipped. "Thank you for being so good with the kids, Firefighter Lyons." She didn't know what else to say. The other two firefighters were putting the equipment away.

"Rafe. And you're welcome. The kids are fun to be

around."

She nodded. "I should get back. I need to supervise lunch."

"I understand."

Brianna turned and walked back into the building, using her badge to unlock the front door. She wanted to stay and chat with Rafe, but she didn't know what to say to him. Another part of her told her to run. Not that it mattered; she'd probably never see him again.

Chapter 2

Rafe walked into Wicked Sanctuary Saturday night at six thirty. Max had called and asked him to come in early to talk. Unsure why he wanted to talk to him, Rafe knocked on Max's office door even though it was open.

"Hey, Rafe," Max said, getting up from his desk and gesturing to the chair in front of it.

"Hi, Max." Rafe sat down in the lush leather chair. "What did you want to talk about?"

Max grinned. "Right to the point." He sat behind his desk. "I've had some members ask about fire cupping."

"You don't allow fire play in the club."

"I don't, but I also never expected people to want it. Just like Anthony's knife play."

"Anthony's knife play is more of a mindfuck. Mine isn't."

"I'm aware." Max leaned forward. "Before we can make any decisions about this, I need to know how much space we would need, safeguards, and if you're willing to be our lead on it."

Rafe sat back. This wasn't something he expected. He'd joined Wicked Sanctuary, knowing fire play wasn't available, but it didn't bother him. "I can help you, but maybe we start with dry cupping first and see how people respond. Fire cupping will definitely mean additional precautions."

"Which is why I wanted to talk with you."

"Can I see the area you want to use?"

"Let's go." Together, they went into the classroom area. "We don't need as much space in here as we used to."

"Membership down?" He thought that might be unusual, but Rafe didn't know for sure.

"No. It's steady. The influx of new members has slowed, and that's fine." Max led him across the room. "I was thinking this area."

Rafe looked around. "How much do you want to keep for classroom space?"

"A twelve-by-twelve room would be fine."

"How big is this now?"

Max frowned. "I'm not sure. I need to ask Zeke or Gabriel, but I believe around eight hundred square feet, maybe more."

He nodded and walked around the room. "First thing is to add some fire-resistant wood work, then fire-resistant paint." Max pulled out his phone and started making notes. "Next would be flooring. I'd recommend Class A vinyl flooring."

"What else?"

"Extra fire extinguishers. Fire blankets, water buckets, wash cloths. Two first aid kits. I'd bring my own cupping equipment." Rafe paused. "I need to check my equipment bag for the rest, but that's the main stuff."

"What kind of table do you need?"

"We can use a massage table covered by fire blankets or wool blankets. And there would need to be a negotiation with the sub and or sub and Dom to do fire cupping. Dry cupping isn't as in depth as I'd do with fire."

"Makes sense. It is Risk Aware Consensual Kink."

"I'm really surprised you're willing to do this." Rafe stared at Max.

"I've never had an issue with it. I wasn't sure if it was needed. Members have been asking, and I have the space, and you're the expert on fire."

Rafe laughed. "I studied under a master." He had. He'd spent years learning from Master Deacon. It also helped that he was a firefighter. He'd been fascinated with fire since he was a kid, so his parents channeled that interest in healthy directions.

"That's the only reason I'm asking; otherwise, I'd tell the members we can't do it. Just like Anthony's knife play. He studied under a master, as well."

"You're worried about injury?" It was smart to think that way.

Max nodded. "I don't want anyone to get hurt. I also want our members to be happy and enjoy the lifestyle."

"Yeah, I can see it."

"There are some things we will never allow. Blood play, needles, bodily fluids."

"I trust you've talked this out with Damon and Jordan." They were Max's partners in the club.

"Yes, and we've talked with our subs, or should I say partners, as well. I wouldn't leave them out of a decision of this magnitude."

"Understandable."

"I'll set up a meeting with Zeke and Gabriel to talk about making the modifications you want. When are you available?"

"Not until toward the end of next week. I work four twelve-hour shifts Monday through Thursday, six in the morning until six at night."

"Got it. Maybe after work on a Thursday night? The club is less crowded, and we won't mess up your days off."

"That works, or anytime on Friday, Saturday, or Sunday. My days off tend to be pretty light for me."

Max nodded. "I'll talk with them and see what we can set up." He glanced up when someone walked into the room.

"Hi, Jordan," Rafe said.

"Rafe." Jordan glanced at Max. "People are starting to arrive."

"I think we're done," Max said.

Rafe nodded. "I'm going to go change." He left the room and went back out to his vehicle to grab his play bag. Having fire play at the club was going to be interesting. His fingers already itched to get started.

* * * *

"You look great," Ellie said.

Brianna looked at herself critically in the full-length bathroom mirror in her apartment. While she'd finished her classes at Wicked Sanctuary over a month ago, she hadn't been able to go to the club. Mainly due to Thanksgiving and Christmas holidays.

The black boy shorts clung to her ass, and her top… Well, she wasn't showing any more than she would at a beach, so why did she feel so naked? "It's fine, I guess."

"You'll knock some of those Doms on their asses."

"I don't want to do that." Brianna gathered up her hair. "What do I do with it?"

"May I braid it?"

"Sure." Brianna sat down, and Ellie made quick work of her hair.

"There, out of the way and easy to loosen." Ellie's phone pinged. "Logan is here."

"Okay." Brianna slipped on a pair of pants, then a shirt, before putting her shoes on. She grabbed the bag that contained her purse, and they walked to the front door. *Keys.* Snatching them off the table, Brianna locked the door.

They climbed into the SUV. Logan leaned over and gave Ellie a brief kiss before glancing at her. "Hi, Brianna."

"Hi, Logan." Since meeting him on Monday, she felt better about letting him drive her to the club. Not that she suspected Logan of anything, it just gave her more peace of mind. "Thanks for the ride."

"No problem." He pulled away from her apartment building. "I was surprised to find out you were a member."

"I couldn't attend much over the holidays, but now that things have calmed down, I want to see what I've gotten myself into."

Logan frowned. "You did go through the classes?"

"Logan." Ellie placed her hand on his arm.

"It's okay. Yes, I did. Noah was my mentor."

"Good man." Logan kept his eyes on the road.

"Forgive him. Doms are always looking out for us," Ellie said.

Brianna nodded, and her heart warmed at Logan's regard. She'd grown up in a loving family, but they'd grown apart when she became an adult. It had to do with a tragedy that struck when she was nine. Her visits at Christmas were still strained even though almost twenty years had passed.

A shiver crawled up her spine. She wouldn't think

about that night. She didn't need to. It was in the past. Six years of therapy had helped her to see that.

All too soon, they were pulling up to Wicked Sanctuary. Once inside, it took her and Ellie no time at all to take off their street clothes and store them before walking out. Brianna admired Ellie's purple and white wristband. Hers was white. A novice. Well, in a way she was.

She'd discovered BDSM years ago before moving to Pleasant Valley. Circumstances prevented her from exploring it. Now, she was ready to delve into the lifestyle she'd heard so much about. The classes Master Max insisted upon were good. They cleared up some misconceptions and, more importantly, made her feel safe in the club.

Hopefully, she wouldn't run into any of her students' parents. That thought sent a chill through her heart. While there wasn't any rule against it in her contract with Pleasant Valley Elementary School, it could make things uncomfortable.

She'd cross that bridge when it happened, if it happened. There was a strict NDA here, so that shouldn't be a problem, right? Brianna sent a look skyward, hoping fate was on her side tonight.

Logan took Ellie's arm and then held his arm out to her. Brianna took a deep breath and slipped her arm through Logan's.

"Shall we, ladies?"

"Yes," Ellie said.

Brianna nodded. They walked to the door being held opened by a man she didn't know, and in they went. She stopped just inside the main room of the club. While she'd been through the classes with Noah, it had been very platonic. The club hadn't been very busy either.

The number of people surprised her. The lighting was low, but not so much she couldn't see where she was going. Hard tech music played in the background. "Unusual music," Brianna commented. All the music she'd heard before had a beat, but wasn't as heavy.

"Not really," Logan answered. "Look to your right, about eleven o'clock."

She did and then saw the flogging scene, the strokes landing in time with the beat of the music. "Oh." Brianna hadn't seen anyone flogged to music before. Her body heated.

"Shall we go into the sub area?" Ellie asked.

"Please." Brianna needed to get her bearings. She'd mainly been in the club on Thursday nights, and it was a lot quieter. Her last class had been on a Friday night, but she'd left before eleven. She was grateful to be able to sit down in the sub area with Ellie.

"I'll be at the bar." Logan swept a kiss over Ellie's lips before walking away.

"Are you okay?" Ellie asked.

"I think so. It's different from class nights." She looked left and right. People everywhere. She wasn't claustrophobic. She just hadn't expected… Brianna took a deep breath. She wasn't afraid but maybe apprehensive.

Her gaze traveled around the club, noting three primary exits and emergency exits. She was pleased to see several fire extinguishers in the club as well. Master Max had told her they had procedures, and they didn't allow an open flame on the play floor. That had relieved her fear of a massive fire.

"Busier. Yes, usually Friday and Saturdays are." Ellie grinned as another woman bounced into the area, wearing a white corset and a thong.

"Hey, Tessa."

"Hi, Ellie." She glanced at Brianna. "Who is your new friend?"

"Brianna, meet Tessa. Her partner is Damon."

"Hi."

"Welcome to the club. I don't remember seeing you around."

"I finished my classes a couple of months ago but haven't been able to come until now."

"Glad you could make it. The holidays are a hard time for people." Tessa smiled.

"Damon on duty?" Ellie asked.

"Yeah. I don't mind. Gives me a chance to talk with everyone. What do you do, Brianna?"

* * * *

Rafe strode into the club with a grin. It felt good to be back. He'd spent some time at Christmas with his parents, then work picked up. He missed the club. He noticed several of the Doms at the bar, Logan included.

Good. Maybe Logan could give him more information on that teacher from their talk at the school. Brianna hadn't left his mind since they'd met. He was attracted to her, but didn't know if she reciprocated. Although she did blush a time or two when he caught her staring at him. Plus, Logan might know if she had any interest in BDSM.

"Hey, Rafe." Logan tapped him on the shoulder.

"How did the talk with Max go?" Jordan asked.

"Good."

"And?" Jordan prompted.

"I'll do it, but only once the modifications are made." He wasn't going to compromise on that. Fire and personal safety first. "I do also want to make sure everyone knows it's RACK."

"I didn't think Max allowed RACK," Dane said, joining the conversation.

Rafe shook Dane's hand. He'd opened an art gallery in town and decided to stay. His partner, Regina, was one of the subs and always made sure to make everyone feel welcome.

"We've been thinking about it," Jordan answered. "Some of the members have an interest in fire play, and Rafe here is an expert in it."

"I wouldn't say expert." Rafe was surprised by Jordan's words.

"I would," Max said, joining the group. "I talked with the master you studied under and still keep up with. Plus, you're a firefighter."

"If anyone knows fire, it's you," Logan commented.

Rafe nodded. He had studied under the best, but it was more than that. The way flames moved, how a fire burned, what caused a fire to start. You name it, he'd studied it.

Some might call it an obsession, but after watching his childhood home burn down, his goal had always been to help others when needed and learning how fire worked, and being a firefighter was a big part of that goal.

"I'll set up something up with Zeke and Gabriel next week, since they both worked on the addition, to see how long it will take to get a room ready. Once that's done, we'll make a general announcement."

"If you want, Max, I can do dry cupping here in the club anytime. That might help give us an idea of how many people want to try fire cupping."

"Dry cupping?" Dane asked.

"Yes. To simplify, it's the same concept, but I use suction rather than fire to help the muscles. It also helps a people decide if they want to actually do fire cupping."

"Sounds intriguing," Logan commented.

"Many find both relaxing. Massage therapists do cupping, and a lot of athletes use it, especially in competition where muscles are strained."

"I bet it's better than a massage," Jordan said, rolling his shoulders.

"It can be. Depends on what you're looking for." Rafe hadn't thought about the Doms wanting to do cupping; he figured it was for the subs. Why he thought that, he didn't know. "I'm open to any Doms who want to try it. Max, before I do any cupping, I want to make sure everyone understands RACK."

"No problem. We can do a demo of dry cupping, and you can explain what you're doing and RACK at the same time."

"So you're changing the rules?" Dane said.

"A little." Max ran his hand through his hair. "I still won't allow blood play, bodily fluids, or needles. Those have way too many bio hazards. After talking with Rafe, we can minimize the fire play risks to the participants, and also to the club."

"I like it," Jordan commented.

Rafe wasn't surprised the Doms liked the idea of it, but he had to wonder about the subs. How many of them would enjoy it? A lot of people did. It helped remove the toxins from the body, but it could also make one feel relaxed and sensual.

"Who's the new sub?" Dane asked, tilting his head toward the area where the subs gathered.

Rafe turned his head, and his eyes opened wide. Brianna? What was she doing here? His heart pounded.

"That's Brianna," Logan said. "She's friends with Ellie."

"She finished her classes with Noah right before Thanksgiving. This is her first time back since before the holidays," Max said.

Rafe kept his gaze on Brianna. She was into kink? This quiet, shy, second grade teacher? He was making assumptions, wild assumptions. Well, maybe not really, she was in a BDSM club, after all. But his body took note of the black sports bra she wore. Another Dom stepped into his field of vision, blocking him from seeing the rest of her outfit, but he'd find out soon enough. Damn. He'd grown hard just staring at her. He needed this woman. In his arms, on his play table, in his bed.

"He's salivating," Jordan said.

Rafe jerked his head around. "I am not." Well, maybe he was. Hard not to with beautiful Brianna sitting in the sub area. Was she ready to play? God, he hoped so.

Everyone laughed, and Rafe shook his head. "Come on, buddy." Logan slapped him on the shoulder. "I'll take you over. It's time I took Ellie around the club."

The pair walked away from the group. "It's not like I need an introduction," Rafe muttered.

"No, but it would make Ellie feel more comfortable, and I bet Brianna too. Remember, she's very new to this."

"I will." *Won't be easy, but I will.* Rafe kept his gaze on Brianna's face as they approached. She chatted with the other subs, and seeing her comfort made him happy. When he and Logan stepped into the space, all talk stopped.

"Ladies," Logan said. "My Ellie, shall we go walk around?"

Ellie glanced at Brianna, who was looking at Rafe. "Sure. Sir."

"Brianna, you remember Rafe?" Logan asked, helping Ellie to her feet.

"I do." Her voice was soft.

Logan eyed her for a long moment, glanced at Rafe, and nodded his head. "Come on, Ellie. Let's go have some fun."

Arm in arm, they walked off. Tess had left a while ago with her Dom, but there were still other subs sitting in the area.

"Brianna, would you allow me the pleasure of your company?" Rafe held his hand out.

He heard the oohs that came from the other subs. "Yes, Sir."

That "yes, Sir" sent a shaft of awareness through his body, almost setting his blood on fire. She placed her hand in his, and he helped her to her feet. "Shall we go into a quiet area and chat?"

Brianna nodded.

Rafe led Brianna over to a smaller area. No one was there right now, so they'd have some privacy. She took one of the overstuffed chairs, so he adjusted the other chair and sat in front of her.

Her gaze darted around the club. Was she nervous or something else? "Brianna," he started. "You don't have to talk with me if you don't want to."

"I want to, Sir."

While the Sir made his skin tingle with anticipation, he had to take things slow for now. "Rafe. Drop the Sir for now."

She nodded, her gaze settling on his face. "I didn't expect to see you here." Her voice was soft.

"Likewise." Rafe glanced at her wrist. Unattached Novice. "How long have you been a member of the club?"

"Not long. I finished my classes up before the holidays, then took a break."

"I took a break during the holidays, as well."

"How long have you been a member?"

"Several years. Did Ellie tell you about the club?"

She stiffened. "I don't want to get her in trouble. I know we're not supposed to talk about…all of this." She waved her hand to encompass the club.

"She's allowed to discuss the club just not the members." He was impressed with Brianna's honesty.

She let out a breath and relaxed against the back of the chair. "The NDA for the club is quite extensive."

"Max likes it that way." It had expanded since he'd joined. Max insisted everyone sign a new one. "What do you know about the lifestyle?"

"A bit." She shifted. "I lived in Seattle before Pleasant Valley and learned some there."

Interesting. "How long have you been in Pleasant Valley?"

"About three years."

"Why did you move from Seattle?"

"I wasn't happy with the school district."

He nodded. "Tell me more about how you got to know the lifestyle." He wanted to get her talking and find out more about her. While he would ask her for permission to look at her questionnaire, he wanted to hear it from her.

"In college, my roommate and her boyfriend were

into kink. I was curious, so she loaned me some books, and we chatted about it."

"What kind of books?"

"BDSM for beginners, BDSM for the novice, Dominance and submission, books on those subjects."

"What did your friend tell you about kink?" Was her friend into safe, sane, and consensual? He thought yes based on the books, considering the actual book *BDSM for the Novice* was written by Max under a pseudonym.

"She told me how everything is consensual. If someone doesn't ask specifically for consent, then a sub should walk away. She also said how relaxing and stress relieving it was for her. She was able to forget about work and just be herself."

"With the right people, the lifestyle is very beneficial." He was glad her roommate had a good experience. So many people didn't.

"Did you go to any clubs in Seattle?"

"I went a couple of times." Her chin lifted, and she crossed her arms over her chest.

"What happened?" By her defensiveness, something had happened.

"It wasn't for me."

She wasn't giving him much. "Tell me more?"

Brianna sighed. "The truth? Most of the men were assholes." Her arms fell to her sides, and she leaned forward. "I felt like shark bait, and it wasn't a good feeling."

"None of the men asked for consent?" It was a guess, but he had a feeling they hadn't.

"Not a single one. After the fifth guy made demands, I walked out. Some of the men's comments to me were not nice."

Rafe's temper flared. "I'm sorry."

"It's not your fault." She waved a hand in the air. "I don't feel that way here."

"Good. Max strives for safe, sane, and consensual."

"With the extensive classes, background checks and stuff, I'm not surprised."

Rafe smiled. "Once in a while, someone will slip through. I've heard Max used to rent out the club to other kink groups, but he stopped the practice after some issues. Max values his club and his members."

"He does. He talked with me at length before he even agreed to let me fill out the paperwork to join. It made me feel safe."

"If you decide you want to hang out with me and I do anything, anything at all, that makes you feel unsafe, tell me. I'm pretty good at reading clues, but we all miss stuff."

"Thank you. I appreciate that."

"Good. Let's talk about limits."

Her eyes widened a bit. "Okay. I'm really new to this, so I have a lot of hard limits."

"Do you have any objection to me looking at your questionnaire?"

"None at all. Am I allowed to look at yours?"

"Of course you are." Rafe glanced around the club. "I see Max by the bar. I'll be right back."

He stood and crossed over to Max, explained what he needed, and Max grinned. "Sure. I'll get them and bring them to you so you can get back to your sub."

"She's not my sub—yet—and I can wait."

"I don't think so." Max pointed in Brianna's direction.

Rafe turned his head. Noah was sitting on the arm of

Brianna's chair and talking with her. Brianna was smiling and chatting happily. Oh no, that was not going to happen. Without a word, Rafe marched over to the pair.

"Rafe," Noah said as he approached.

"Noah." Rafe took a seat in the chair across from Brianna.

Noah stood. "Great chatting with you, Brianna."

"You too. Thanks for the words of encouragement."

Noah gave Rafe a hard look before walking away. "What was that about?" Rafe asked.

"Noah was my mentor/trainer. He was checking up on me; that's all."

"Then why…" Rafe shook his head. Max liked to meddle in the budding relationships of his members. Where he found the time, Rafe didn't know. "I'm glad it was Noah. He's very gentle."

"And you aren't?" Brianna grinned at him. "I saw you with the kids. You're sweet, gentle, and patient."

"Hey, I have a reputation to uphold." There was laughter in his voice.

"Here you go," Max said and handed Rafe and Brianna each a folder. "Just give them back to me when you're done."

"Thanks, Max." Rafe stared at Brianna. "Our questionnaires. Shall we read them and then chat some more?"

"Sure."

Rafe settled back in his chair and opened the file.

* * * *

Brianna stared at the folder. Why did she feel like she was having trouble holding her own with Rafe? Maybe it was because she'd been so surprised to see him in Wicked Sanctuary. Her reaction to him wasn't normal for her. Was she ready for this?

Yes, she decided. Ellie trusted Rafe; otherwise, she never would have allowed Logan to introduce Rafe to Brianna. She opened the folder and skimmed over his application and faltered when she reached fire under sensation play.

Fire play was checked off. Brianna vaguely remembered Max mentioning fire play wasn't part of the offerings when she signed up. Not that she cared. Fire was not her thing. Fire never would be her thing. Ever.

She bit her lip to keep a bitter laugh from bursting free. Her gut clenched. Was she really going to get involved with a firefighter? Everything inside her told her to get up, tell him she was sorry, and leave.

Yet she still sat here, focused on what she was feeling. Excitement, apprehension, desire, hope. Hope? Yep, hope was there. Hope she'd found someone who would allow her to be herself.

Rafe would understand if she wasn't interested in fire play. Plus, she had nothing against firefighters, one had saved her when she was a child. She'd never know if BDSM was for her if she didn't try with Rafe. That's what she was here for. Fire play didn't have to be included in their time in the club.

Brianna took a breath and finished reading his questionnaire. She closed the folder to find Rafe staring at her. "Is there something wrong?"

"No. A question. You put a hard limit on fire play, may I know why?"

"It's not something I'm interested in." That was the only answer she was willing to give at the moment.

He nodded.

"If we're not compatible, that's okay." A dagger

made its way into her heart as she said the words. At this moment, she couldn't see doing anything in the club unless it was with Rafe.

His green eyes darkened. "We're compatible."

Brianna nodded. She thought so too. While there had only been a couple of questions and reading, her nerves were wound tight over the negotiations. Her mood lightened, and she giggled. What made her think it would be easy?

"What was that giggle for?"

"I was thinking how negotiations were harder than I thought."

"They are never easy in the beginning. Neither one of us wants to make a mistake." He shifted her folder from one hand to the other. "Let's give these back to Max and then walk around for a bit and talk some more."

"I'd like that." It would give her nerves time to calm down.

"May I have your permission to touch you if we stop and watch any scenes?"

"Yes." She could handle touching.

"Thank you. Protocols are back in place now." He stood and held his hand out to her.

"Yes, Sir." She allowed him to help her from the chair, and he kept his arm around her waist as they walked across the room to where Max sat at the bar. Sierra was standing between Max's legs, and he had his arms around her waist.

"Thanks, Max," Rafe said, handing him Brianna's file. Brianna relinquished Rafe's, as well.

"You're welcome. Honey, would you run these back to the office for me?"

"Yes, Sir." Max kissed Sierra's temple before she

took the folders and left.

"All good, Brianna?" Max asked.

"I'm fine, Master Max." Brianna wondered why he was asking.

Max nodded but stared at Rafe.

"We'll be fine," Rafe said, before leading her away.

"What was that about?" There was something about the exchange that bothered her.

"Max being Max. He's protective of all the subs."

"And what does that have to do with us?" She was a sub, but she wasn't completely uninformed, and Max knew this.

"He's just making sure you're comfortable with me. Max is aware your hard limit is fire play."

"Oh." Her eyes widened. "But you've accepted that, haven't you?"

"I have."

"Then I don't see the problem." Besides, it wasn't available in the club anyway, so she didn't have anything to worry about.

"Sir," he said gently.

"Sir," she answered, shaking her head. She'd forgotten so fast.

Rafe tipped her head up until her eyes met his gaze. "It's all right. We're just beginning. Don't berate yourself for slips."

That simple statement rolled through Brianna like warm cocoa. He cared for her peace of mind.

"No punishments. Yet."

She might have freaked out a bit, but the laughter in his eyes brought a smile to her face. Rafe crooked his elbow for her to slip her hand through, then he rested his other hand atop hers on his arm. This felt comfortable.

Good. Right. Brianna smiled up at him.

A few hours later, she and Rafe were back in the quiet area. It was nice to walk around and see the different scenes and who was in the scene. Doms and subs of different sizes, nationalities, and communication styles.

She knew communication was important, but it really showed tonight. He'd kept it very casual. He would run his fingers up and down her arms, over her bare abdomen, the back of her neck. Each touch made her skin heat, and she was surprised how strongly she reacted to his touch. It wasn't like someone hadn't touched her like that before.

"Would you be okay sitting in my lap while we talk?"

"Yes, Sir." That was one thing she was still getting used to. Consent. If he was doing something they hadn't talked about, he would ask her permission. If they continued on together, and she suspected they would, she would tell him that, unless it was pushing a soft limit, he had blanket consent. She'd not left even one blank spot on her questionnaire.

Rafe sat and pulled her gently onto his lap. That was another thing. He kept his touch and gestures soft and gentle, as if he was afraid of hurting her. It warmed her heart, but she wasn't a fragile flower. "I'm not glass, Sir."

"Oh?" His eyes gleamed in the low light. "Are you saying you want me to be rough?"

She bit her lip. "No. It's just…" Lord, she had no idea how to say this, and hesitation wasn't like her. How had Rafe made her lose words like this?

His fingers trailed from her temple over her cheek to her shoulder. "What did you mean?"

Brianna closed her eyes and gathered her thoughts. "If we're going to continue after tonight, you don't have to ask for consent on everything, Sir. If you're going to push my soft limits, then ask. Talking about what we'll do before a scene also. But that's really it."

"I see. After tonight, I'll take that into consideration. But you have the power to revoke consent at any time, okay?"

"That's acceptable, Sir." She relaxed against him.

"Good. What did you see tonight that you'd like to try?"

"Tall order, Sir." It was. "The bondage scene was interesting, as was the flogging scene."

"You didn't like the web?"

"Web?" It took her a minute to remember which one that was. "Oh, that one, Sir. It looks uncomfortable, and I wouldn't want to be spun around."

Rafe nodded. "What was interesting about the bondage and flogging scenes?"

Another tall order. Brianna took a breath and let it out. She hadn't talked with a man like this before. Not even when she'd played a little bit in the Seattle clubs. Initial negotiations, but that had been it.

"The bondage scene looked so sensual, Sir." It had. The Dom and sub were great together. "I liked how Dom Dane took his time with Regina, Sir. He didn't rush anything."

"A good Dom doesn't rush. He makes sure his sub feels every touch, every tingle of excitement. What about the flogging scene?"

A shiver went up her spine. "Is it always so sensual, Sir?" That was the only word she could think of at the moment.

"Depending on the couple, it can be." He shifted and tightened his arm around her shoulder. "What made it seem sensual to you?"

"The way Dom Damon touched Tessa. He checked in with her often and…" How to explain this? "There was something in her eyes, something more than love, Sir."

His lips turned up. "They've been together for a while now, and yes, they're in love."

"It shows, Sir."

"As it should. You'll see that between several couples here, but you'll also see satisfaction and pleasure."

Brianna nodded. She'd never really observed scenes at the club in Seattle, but then again, Seattle had been more about hooking up and not necessarily about embracing the lifestyle and all it had to give.

"My next question: Would you like to try anything tonight?"

Chapter 3

Brianna blinked. Did she want to scene with Rafe? *Hell, yeah*, her body yelled. *Wait, what did he have planned*, her mind countered. She hadn't expected things to progress this fast. Or had she? Her body was already anticipating his hands on her more than they already had been.

"What do you have in mind, Sir?"

"How do you feel about a little sensation play?"

She'd been super curious about that and had marked it as a soft limit—labeled number one—after asking Max about it. He explained anything with a one meant you were willing to try, two, three and four would be fully negotiated, five was a hard limit. "What would you use, Sir?"

"For tonight, a feather to see how you react to it, along with my touch."

"I'd like that, Sir."

Rafe smiled. "Let me see what's available." He slipped her off his lap and onto the sofa with little effort.

Brianna was surprised. While she was small, she wasn't that small, yet he handled her like she weighed nothing. She watched Rafe cross the room, admiring the way his leather pants cupped his ass. She'd never really liked leather pants on a man…until now.

He talked with Jordan, then nodded, and made his way back to her. His grin was infectious, and Brianna couldn't help smiling at him.

"The bondage table is available, but I won't restrain you. Not tonight, anyway."

Heat hit her body, and her skin flushed. Rafe helped her stand and then led her to the small stage where one of the bondage tables sat. Her heart pounded as he helped her up onto the stage and over to the table. "Are you okay?"

"Fine, Sir."

He nodded. "Let me help you onto the table." Putting his hands on her waist, he lifted her.

It was a bit disconcerting how he could pick her up so easily, then she remembered he was a firefighter and in tip-top shape. Once her butt was on the table, he helped her lay face down.

She turned her head so she could see him. Jordan dropped a bag on the stage, and Rafe thanked him. Rafe picked up the bag and set it on a nearby table, then walked to the edge of the stage, took a couple of blankets from a sub, and put them on the table, as well.

Rafe unzipped his bag. The noise the zipper made sounded loud to her. Brianna closed her eyes, took a deep breath, and let it out, then did so again. Her muscles relaxed. When she opened her eyes, Rafe was there.

"Nervous?"

"A bit, Sir." She'd never done sensation play before. It sounded odd, but she'd never trusted someone enough to allow them to tease her skin. She trusted Rafe. It was an instinctual thing. They'd only met twice. He didn't act like some of the Doms in the Seattle club. All full of themselves. Rafe was all about consent and making sure she was comfortable.

"I'm only going to use feathers and my hands."

"Yes, Sir."

"Can you close your eyes for me?"

She swallowed. "Yes, Sir." Her lashes fell, and darkness descended. It wasn't uncomfortable, just different. She couldn't see, so instead, she concentrated on her hearing. The music playing in the background, the murmur of voices, the occasional swish of a flogger, the soft cry of a sub in pleasure.

"Someone is in their head." His voice was soft as he touched her arms and placed them where he wanted them. His finger trailed down her arm to her palm and fingers, before it disappeared, only to reappear on her upper thigh. "Spread your legs a little, please."

Brianna's heart pounded harder as she slipped her legs apart. How far could this go?

"Perfect," he said, before dropping a kiss on the small of her back.

It was then Brianna realized he hadn't asked her to remove her clothes. That was a surprise. She fully expected him to. Anticipation hummed in her blood as she waited for his touch.

Something soft touched her shoulder, and she jumped.

"Easy," Rafe whispered.

The softness trailed over her skin. Soft and silky was the only way she could describe it. He continued down her body and then slid it over her feet, and she giggled.

"Ticklish?" He twirled the feathers over the soles of feet.

"A bit, Sir."

"Noted." He shifted the feather, and now his fingers

followed it up her body. His touch was light. Her nerves were alive with every swipe of the feather and then his touch. Inch by inch, she sank into the emotion, letting her mind go and just feeling.

* * * *

Rafe grinned when Brianna finally relaxed. She had been so tense, but now he saw her body sink into the soft leather of the table. He set the starburst feather tickler aside and picked up the Ostrich one.

The starburst was smaller and more concentrated. The Ostrich was softer and might be a little bit more ticklish, but he'd see. Brianna's skin was creamy smooth, and he enjoyed the way it blushed beneath his touch.

Did she even realize her skin was flushing with arousal? He started with her shoulders again, and went up and down her body several times before he moved it up the inside of her legs to her inner thighs.

"Ohhh." She shifted on the table.

"Tickle?"

"No, a different sensation, Sir."

Every time she said Sir, his dick pulsed. Funny, he hadn't reacted to a woman like this before. He'd had relationships in the past, long-term ones. Well, if a year or two was considered long-term.

Oddly, he'd even scened with a couple of the subs here in the club and never felt such a powerful attraction or need to be with them as he did with Brianna. It didn't make sense. They'd just met each other.

He shook his head. He'd figure it out eventually, just like he did with fire. All it took was finding the patterns, seeing the movement, and other things. Tossing the feather tickler aside, he ran his palms over Brianna's skin, loving the feel of it against his own.

Jordan waved at him. Damn, their time was almost up. He'd been lucky enough to be able to squeeze in between other scenes. Slowly, he wound down the scene, keeping his touch light and more infrequent until he stopped.

"Brianna."

"Yeah." Her voice was soft and dreamy. Oh yes, he'd helped her relax, totally and completely.

He smiled. "The scene is over."

"Oh." She didn't move.

Jordan climbed onto the stage. "Give her a minute."

Rafe nodded, put his toys into his bag, and took it back to his cubby by the bar. When he returned, Jordan was still standing there, and Brianna hadn't moved.

"I don't think she's back with us yet," Jordan commented.

"Subspace from light sensation play?" Rafe was surprised.

"Maybe. More like she's so relaxed she doesn't want to move." Jordan looked from Brianna and back to him. "My suggestion is to cover her with a blanket, have her roll on her side, pick her up, and carry her over to the aftercare area. I can clean up the table for you."

"Thanks." It wasn't as if Rafe didn't know how to take care of a sub; he'd just never had one react like Brianna. Most would hop off the table within five minutes, telling him they were refreshed and happy.

"By the way, Logan and Ellie had to leave. Apparently, Ellie has a party tomorrow."

Rafe nodded, grabbed a blanket, and shook it open. "Brianna. I'm going to lay a blanket over you, then I want you to roll onto your right side toward me."

"Yes, Sir." Her voice was still very soft.

He placed the blanket over her, and she did as he asked. Rafe bent his knees, put his arms under her, and lifted.

"Goodness," she commented as she put an arm around his neck. "I'm too heavy."

That was the second time she said something about being heavy. "You are perfect." She was. She fit into his arms. With care, he maneuvered them off the small stage and into the aftercare area.

He sat down on a sofa with her in his arms, making sure her legs were resting on the cushions. Hannah, one of the subs, walked by. "Hannah, would you be able to grab me two bottles of water from the bar, please."

"Of course, Sir." Hannah moved across the room and back within a few minutes. "Here you go, Sir." She set the bottles on the side table where he could reach them. "Noah loosened the tops already."

"Thank you, Hannah. I appreciate you doing this."

Hannah blushed and flittered away.

Rafe glanced at Brianna to see her eyes were open, and she was watching him.

"Hey, beautiful. How are you doing?"

"I feel like I've had a fully body massage, Sir." Her voice was stronger now.

Interesting reaction. "Do you need some water?" Some subs were dehydrated after scenes.

"Yes, please, Sir."

Always so polite. And while it was protocol, he couldn't wait to see if he could make her less polite and even lose her cool. Grabbing one of the bottles, he twisted the lid off and carefully held it to her lips. She sat up a little bit, and lifted her hand to take the bottle.

He kept his hand on it just in case she had an issue.

Not that he expected her to, but he was going to make sure she was taken care of.

"Thank you." When she lowered the bottle, it was half gone. "I didn't realize how thirsty I was, Sir."

"Drop the Sir, for now." He took the bottle from her, put the cap on, and set it back on the table. "Coming back into your body?"

"Yes. I've had full-body massages, but this felt so different."

"How so?"

"It was more sensual. I've never relaxed that fast or hard. When you were done, I didn't want to move."

"I'm glad you felt that way."

She smiled at him. "It was a surprise; that's for sure. Especially when you picked me up. I didn't expect that."

"Any good Dom will take care of his sub."

"Is that what I am? Your sub?"

"I would like you to be." He wasn't going to pressure her.

"I need to think on it."

"Of course."

"Are you always this agreeable?"

Rafe laughed. "Not always."

"I don't know what time it is." She glanced around.

"No clocks in here," he reminded her.

"I was looking for Ellie or Logan."

"They left." Her face fell. Her mouth opened then shut. "I suspect they saw us in the scene, plus Jordan told me Logan said something about a party Ellie is doing tomorrow."

"Damn, that's right."

"I can drive you home if you wish, or I'll find you a ride."

"I would appreciate you giving me a ride home."

"Thank you." Her trust in him humbled him. "Let me know when you're ready to go."

She nodded and relaxed into his arms.

* * * *

It felt nice to be held in Rafe's arms. Brianna was a little surprised that Ellie left without saying anything, but then, she'd been in a scene with Rafe. At first, she was a little hurt, but she trusted Ellie and Logan to know she would be safe with Rafe.

Not only that, she trusted him, as well. She'd better after that scene. Oh man, that scene. Her skin still tingled from the sensations he'd created with only feathers and his touch.

Brianna had never felt that way with any man, in or out of the lifestyle. Rafe's touch heated her body and made her want things she'd never thought about. She shifted and yawned. It was getting late, and while she didn't have work tomorrow, it was time to go home.

"I think it's time to go."

He nodded and lifted her as he stood. Damn, this man was strong. Rafe set her on her feet but kept his arm around her waist. "Is there anyone you need to say good-bye to?"

"I'm good." She was just getting to know the other subs. Rafe guided her out of the club and to the ladies' room. "Meet you here."

She nodded and slipped into the bathroom. Thankfully, it was empty. She wasn't sure if she wanted to talk with anyone, and she quickly pulled on her street clothes and grabbed her purse. Rafe was leaning against the wall when she walked out.

Damn, he'd put on a t-shirt that molded to those

muscles of his. He held a black bag in his hand.

"I hope you weren't waiting long."

"No. Max wanted to chat for a minute."

"Is everything okay?"

"Fine." Rafe took her by the elbow and escorted her out to the parking lot. He led her over to a deep maroon-colored SUV. A big one.

She shook her head.

"What?" he asked.

"What is it with men and huge SUVs?"

"Probably because we are always hauling stuff around for parties, camping, and other things." He tossed his bag in the back, then opened the passenger door. "Plus, we get to do this." He grasped her by the waist and lifted her into the vehicle.

Brianna giggled. "I never thought of that." She fastened her seatbelt after he shut the door.

"Where do you live?" he asked.

She gave him the address and fell silent. It was a comfortable silence, something she hadn't experienced with a man in a while. When he pulled up in front of her apartment building, she reached for the door handle.

"Stay there," he ordered and climbed out. She gave him a hard stare when he opened her door, put his hands on her waist, and helped her out of his vehicle. "I didn't mean my words to be so brisk."

"Okay." Her ire fled.

He kept his arm around her waist as he guided her to the front of the building. Brianna pulled out her keys and unlocked the common door. "Thank you for tonight."

"Please allow me to escort you to your apartment."

"All right." She really didn't need an escort, but he'd asked rather than ordered. They made their way down the hall. Her apartment was the last one, next to the emergency exit.

"Thank you again," she said after opening her door.

"May I have your number?"

Another ask. "Sure. It's..." She rattled off her number. A minute later, her cell rang inside her purse.

"Now, you have mine." He put his phone back in his pocket. "If you start feeling teary or sad, please call me. It can happen after a scene."

"I will." She didn't think she'd gone into subspace, so she didn't expect it to happen. She glanced up at him, and he was watching her.

"I'm going to kiss you now." He waited a second before he lowered his head. His lips brushed against hers. Soft and sweet, once then twice before he lifted his head. "Good night, Brianna. Go inside and lock the door behind you."

"Night, Rafe." She slipped inside, shut and locked the door. His kiss had been nice and gentle. She hadn't been expecting that.

With a sigh, she pushed away from the door and made her way into her bedroom. She'd dream about that kiss and his touch. Undressing and doing her nightly routine, her mind wandered over the night's activities.

She and Rafe fit. That was all she could think about. They'd hit it off, and he'd been able to get her to relax. It had been nice.

Brianna crawled into bed and laid there. Sleep was a long time coming, and when she did finally fall asleep, she dreamed of Rafe.

Chapter 4

Rafe drove home with a smile on his face. Brianna had been so responsive to him. Luckily, he hadn't screwed things up when he ordered her to stay in the car. He hadn't meant to bark it out like that. Usually he had more finesse.

She disarmed him, and his dominant side had taken over without thought. He would need to tread carefully with Brianna. The scene with her had been damn hot. His dick hadn't settled down at all. She had no idea how beautiful she was.

Pulling into his driveway, he hit the remote to his garage door and drove in. He was so glad he'd bought this house. Luck had been on his side with it. He'd always lived pretty frugally, so when this new complex came up for sale, he'd jumped on it before the prices went too high.

Having been early into the process, he was able to get the house customized. It had cost him a little more, but he was happy with it. Of course, Zeke and Gabriel, fellow Doms and the best construction guys around, had cut him a break too. After closing the garage door, he grabbed his bag out of the back and walked into the house.

He didn't bother to turn on any lights. In his bedroom, he dropped his bag on the floor and went into the bathroom. With a flip of the handle, he turned on the shower. Setting the timer on the fan to keep the excess moisture out of the room, he stripped, and his cock sprang free of its confinement.

In the shower, Rafe ducked his head under the water, lathered up his hands, then took his cock in his palm. He groaned as he stroked himself. Brianna's body came into focus as he closed his eyes and pictured her breathless sighs as he used the feathers and touched her silky skin. With each pass, she had relaxed until she was like a puddle on the table. It pleased him that she trusted him enough to allow herself to relax. His balls tightened, and his dick pulsed as he came.

He panted and braced his arms against the shower wall. Was it way too early to be thinking about fucking Brianna? They'd just barely started, but his cock didn't care.

He saw a lot of showers in his future.

* * * *

The next morning after his workout, Rafe picked up his cell and pulled up Brianna's number.

"Hello."

"Good morning, Brianna. Rafe here. How are you feeling?"

"Good morning. I feel great."

"No sadness or feeling any need to cry?"

"None at all. I didn't hit subspace last night."

"I'm aware. I only want to make sure you're okay. We've never scened together before."

"Thank you. I do appreciate your caring."

"Would you like to go to the club with me next weekend?" Her silence told him she wasn't expecting him to ask that question. Or maybe she didn't know how to tell him no.

"I would."

He grinned. It wasn't a no. "Why don't we go to dinner before the club on Friday night? I'd like to know more about you."

"Don't you have to work?"

"I work four twelve-hour shifts with Friday, Saturday, and Sunday as my days off."

"Fridays are usually light for me, and I leave school at four."

"I'll pick you up at six; that will give us time to eat, talk, and get to the club before it gets too busy."

"I can meet you." There was a small hesitation in her voice. He wouldn't have caught it if he hadn't been listening so closely.

"You can, but then what would we do with your car? I can't see leaving it at the restaurant or the club."

"You don't think I'll be fit to drive?"

"Not if I have my way." While he probably shouldn't be so honest, he wanted to gauge her reaction.

"You can pick me up for dinner, and then we'll see about driving me home."

A compromise he could live with. "Deal. Have a good Sunday and rest of your week."

"Wait," she said. "What restaurant on Friday?"

"Anything you don't like to eat?" He'd been thinking lots of protein as they would both need it.

"I'm pretty flexible."

"You don't have to dress up."

"You're not going to tell me where?"

"Nope." A little surprise wouldn't hurt her. "Until Friday, my lady." Rafe disconnected the call. It was going to be a long week.

* * * *

His words were true.

By Thursday evening, Rafe was ready for a day off. "What a week," he said to Tim, a fellow firefighter.

"No kidding. I'm glad it's over."

"Don't jinx us," Frank, their captain, said.

"Not trying to." Rafe was happy to work with Frank and Tim. They'd been together several years. It was imperative to trust the men and women you worked with in this job.

"I need a shower," Tim said.

"Don't we all." Rafe put his equipment away in his locker, grabbed a clean set of clothes, and headed for the showers.

"Any big plans for the weekend?" Tim asked in the large communal shower.

"Nothing major." Rafe wasn't ready to talk about Brianna with his co-workers yet. He wanted to see where the relationship went. He almost laughed. They didn't have a relationship yet. Heck, they hadn't even had a date, but that would be resolved tomorrow.

Finishing up his shower, he dressed and grabbed his bag. "Rafe," Frank called his name as he was walking toward the back door.

"What's up?"

"Come into my office for a second."

Rafe frowned. What could the captain want? He walked into the office, and Frank closed the door.

"Stop frowning. Nothing is wrong," Frank said.

"I'm racking my brain over why you wanted to chat with me."

"I wanted to let you know Paula and I are going to be at the club this weekend. I didn't want to surprise you."

"No worries." Rafe was the one who told Frank about the club. Somehow they hadn't been there at the same time yet.

"Good. We've been so busy but we both miss the club and need a good night for ourselves."

"Enjoy. I'll be there, as well." Rafe opened the door and walked out. He didn't mind his boss being at the club. He'd run into a lot of people he saw outside the club. Pleasant Valley wasn't too small, but it seemed if you went to the Sweet & Savory café, you'd eventually run into someone from the club.

Once home, he called the Double D BBQ and checked on his reservation for tomorrow night. A habit of his to make sure everything was set up. Once assured of the reservation, Rafe called for pizza. He didn't feel like cooking.

By the time he ate, he was yawning. Not surprising. He worked six in the morning to six in the evenings, and today had been non-stop. Sitting on his sofa, beer on the side table, he found a movie to watch and within minutes was asleep.

* * * *

Brianna smiled as the last of her students hopped in the bus. She walked back to her classroom. Thank goodness it was Friday. She'd been distracted all week by thoughts of Rafe. The man had found a way under her skin. Under, over, and soon, hopefully, inside.

"Any weekend plans?" Ruby asked.

"Nothing special." Ruby was one the other teachers, and they were friendly, but she wasn't about to tell anyone at school about the club. That was her private business. "What about you?"

"Nothing. Just going out for drinks with some

girlfriends. Why don't you come with us?"

"I'd love to, but I have a previous engagement."

"Oh." Ruby's eyes twinkled. "Who is he?"

Brianna's face heated. "A friend." That was all she was ready to say.

"Sounds interesting. Have fun. And I want to hear all about it on Monday." Ruby waved as she left, and Brianna flopped down in her chair.

Have fun. Those two words bounced around in her head. She wondered what Rafe had planned for tonight. Not that the man would tell her. She'd texted him last night, trying to get more information out of him.

He hadn't answered until this morning, all apologetic, saying he fell asleep early. He would pick her up at six, and he couldn't wait to see her. His words made her skin tingle and her heart pound.

She shook her head and tidied up her desk, grabbed her messenger bag, and walked out to her car. Once home, she dropped her bag by the kitchen table but pulled out her wallet and cell phone.

No text from Rafe. She hoped he was having a good day off. Going into her bedroom, she gazed at her clothes. Not that she had a large amount. He said casual for dinner. She grabbed a pair of black jeans and a purple top.

Pulling a small carry bag out of her closet, she put her club clothes and shoes in it. Then she pulled out one of her small purses. It wasn't big enough for her wallet, but she put some money, a credit card, and her cell in it.

She glanced at the clock. Forty-five minutes before Rafe arrived. She could take a quick shower and be ready in that time.

Forty minutes later, the buzzer in her apartment went

off, letting her know there was someone at the front door. "Yes," she said into the speaker.

"It's Rafe."

"Be right down." She clicked off and picked up her small purse, bag for the club, and her keys. Exhilaration flowed through her veins as she walked down the hall. Rafe stood by the door, looking delicious in his jeans and polo top.

"Hi," she said as she pushed the door open.

"Hi." He took her bag out of her hand. "Why didn't you buzz me in?"

His tone held annoyance. "I'm sorry, old habit." As a kid, someone had been buzzed into the apartment building where she lived who shouldn't have been there. The results had been tragic.

She shook her head. Those memories had no place being there tonight. Brianna wanted to enjoy her time with Rafe.

"Next time, I'd prefer if you'd buzz me in so I'm able to escort you." He put her bag in the back of his vehicle with his, then helped her into the passenger seat. Her skin tingled from his touch.

She glanced at him when he climbed into the driver's seat. "I will."

"Thank you." He leaned over and brushed a kiss on her cheek. "I hope you're hungry."

"Are you going to tell me where we're going?"

"Nope." He grinned at her before he pulled out of the apartment parking lot and onto the street.

Brianna laughed. "Keeping me in suspense."

"Anticipation is part of the game."

His words caused a shiver of pleasure to slide over her skin. Oh, she was anticipating their time in the club tonight. She had been all week.

"How was your week?" she asked.

"Busy. How about yours?"

"Not bad. The kids were still excited about your and Logan's visit last week."

"Your kids are great."

"They're really not mine, but thank you." Her gaze fell on the restaurant's sign. "Double D BBQ." It wasn't too far from where she lived.

"I thought it would be good for our first date."

"Is that what this is?"

"For me, yes."

Brianna allowed herself a slight smile. Good to know.

Rafe parked, and they went into the restaurant. The hostess took them to a booth in the corner, handed them menus, and left.

She'd been here before and loved the food. "This is a great choice."

"I'm glad. You've eaten here before?"

"Who hasn't?" She grinned before picking up her menu. What was she in the mood for?

"Good evening, Rafe, Brianna," Mike, their waiter, said, coming up to the table.

Rafe stared at her. "You must come here a lot to be on first name basis."

She bit her lip. Rafe sounded jealous. "Mike's baby sister is in my class." Brianna glanced at the waiter. "How are you doing, Mike?"

"Good. What can I get you to drink?"

"Water for now," she said.

"I'll have iced tea," Rafe replied.

"Great. I'll have those right out to you along with

bread." Mike walked away.

Brianna closed her menu and stared at Rafe. "How often do you come here?"

"Probably once a month. What does it matter?"

"Rafe, do you know how you sound right now?" It was a tone she didn't like.

He blinked, then shook his head. "Sorry. I'm acting out of character."

"I don't think so." She lowered her voice. "I think the dominant in you is claiming something he believes is his." Rafe's eyes widened, and Brianna laughed. "I work with kids. I'm good at observation."

He set his menu down and reached over and captured her hand. "Does it turn you off?"

She had to think for a moment. "Not really. I kind of like your protectiveness."

He grinned.

"But not all the time. I know a lot of people in the community due to my job."

"Noted. I'll behave myself in public."

"In public only?" Where were these questions coming from? His eyes sparked with desire.

"In the club or bedroom, you are mine."

A shiver of anticipation slid up her spine. She was so ready for this. Mike returned with their drinks and bread, and took their orders.

"There's extra cornbread in there for you, Brianna," Mike said before leaving.

"You have him wrapped around your pinky," Rafe said.

"He knows I love their cornbread." She plucked a piece out of the basket and put it on the bread plate. Breaking off a fragment, she popped it into her mouth, closed her eyes, and groaned. It was still warm.

Rafe made a strange noise, and she opened her eyes.

"Are you okay?" she asked.

"Do you know how hard I am right now?"

Heat flared deep in her belly and spread. "No." What else could she say?

He took her hand and placed it over his groin. Brianna inhaled sharply at the hardness beneath her palm.

"I've been this way since last Saturday night."

"I feel like I should apologize, but another part me is glad you're hurting like I am."

Heat flared in his eyes. "Damn it, if we weren't in public…" He glanced around, then took her lips in a hard and fast kiss.

She could barely breathe after the kiss. She wanted more. This wasn't like her at all. She liked taking her time getting to know a man before she slept with him, but with Rafe, she wanted him in her bed.

It was too soon though. Logically she knew that. She pulled her hand away from his hardness. "Tell me how you became a firefighter." That would take her mind off her need for him. Maybe.

Chapter 5

Rafe sat back at Brianna's question. She was right to bring him down from the sensual haze that had surrounded them. They were in a public restaurant, after all. He blew out a breath. "I've always been fascinated by fire."

She shivered. "Really?"

"Yes." Mike arrived with their dinner and more cornbread and left. "Let's eat." After a few minutes, he glanced at her. "Why did you become a teacher?"

Brianna was quiet for minute. "I like teaching, and kids are fun in second grade. Their minds are usually very open and ready to learn."

"You said you moved to Pleasant Valley from Seattle a few years ago. Where did you grow up?"

"Oregon."

"You're a Pacific Northwest native?"

She laughed. "Not really. I lived in Oregon for a few years. Before that, I worked back East. I got my degree from Maryland University. What about you?"

"I've lived in Washington all my life. In different cities, of course."

"That must have been nice."

"I was lucky. Family?"

"My parents live in Florida now and enjoy their life there."

"No siblings?"

"No." Her gaze slid away from his and to her plate.

Rafe wondered about that, but he wouldn't ask more right now. He didn't want to make her sad.

"I'm sorry. I have two younger sisters."

Brianna coughed and took a drink of her water. "Your sisters must love your protectiveness."

Rafe heard the sarcasm in her voice and grinned. "Not really, but they tolerate it when I see them."

They finished eating, and Rafe paid the bill over Brianna's objection.

"I like paying my own way," she said.

"I'm a little old-fashioned and prefer to pay for my date's meal."

She sighed as he helped her into his SUV. Once they were on the road to the club, she turned to him. "What is going to happen tonight?"

"What would you like to happen?" He wanted her to tell him what she was expecting. He'd played with subs but had never had a full-time relationship with one, and that's what he wanted with Brianna.

"I really enjoyed what you did last week."

"I'm glad. How much further do you want to take it?" He didn't want to push her, not yet.

"I'm not sure." She shifted. "Give me some ideas of what you'd like to try."

"You know this is for your pleasure, not mine."

"But I want you to have pleasure, as well."

"Thank you." Brianna was so giving; that's probably what made her a good teacher. "How would you feel tonight going topless in a scene?"

"I think I can do that."

"Good. I'll use a feather again and play with your breasts and nipples. After that, we'll see how you feel."

"That works."

Rafe turned into the driveway of the club, punched in the gate code, and parked. He helped Brianna out, then grabbed their bags. Once they signed in, he watched her go into the women's bathroom, and he went into the men's. Thankfully, he could change quicker than she could.

* * * *

Brianna went to an open locker and put her purse inside, then set her bag on the bench. A sob echoed through the room. "Hello," she called out.

"I'm fine," came a shaky voice.

She followed the voice and found Emily, one of the subs, sitting on the bench by the toilets. "Emily, what's wrong?" Brianna sat down and put her arm around Emily's shoulders.

"It's nothing. I'm just being over emotional."

"I don't believe that. Do you want me to go get someone?"

"No," Emily yelled. "See? Over emotional."

Something had happened. Brianna persisted. "I'm here." She squeezed Emily. "It sometimes helps to talk about it." Brianna racked her brain to remember if Emily had a partner. During her last class, she'd been introduced to a lot of the subs and their partners.

"I don't want Master Max involved."

Red flags went up. Brianna was aware Max was very protective of all the subs, regardless of gender. "I can't say I won't involve Master Max, but I can say I won't tell him unless I think others might be in danger." She could live with that compromise.

"You haven't played much here, have you?"

"Not really. Holidays and all."

"The holidays are pretty quiet around here, and that's

53

fine. I don't have family close, and it's hard for me to travel and see them, so I like coming to the club."

Brianna nodded. "I can understand that."

"Master Max closed the club for Christmas and New Year, and normally, that isn't an issue."

"But this year it was."

"I was feeling lonely. And I'd met a Dom here at the club. He's been a member, and I didn't see any red flags."

"But?" Brianna knew something had happened.

"We went to coffee and dinner a few times, and then he asked me to a New Year's Eve party. I accepted." Brianna nodded, and Emily continued, "When the party was over…" Emily let out a hiccup as fresh tears ran down her face.

"Did he force you?"

Emily nodded.

Brianna took a deep breath. "Is he here in the club tonight?"

"Yes. I saw him the minute I walked in, and I ran out."

"I don't blame you." Brianna stood and grabbed one of the tissue boxes sitting by the sink and took it to Emily. "I know you don't want to involve Master Max, but we need to. What he did was a crime."

"How? We were dating."

"I don't give a damn if you were married. He violated your trust and you."

"I guess." Emily wiped her face.

"What is his name?" Brianna kept her tone calm even though rage flowed through her veins.

"Ward."

"I'll be right back." Brianna stood, grateful she was

still dressed. She marched out of the bathroom.

"Brianna?" Rafe straightened from where he was leaning against the wall.

"Give me a minute." She didn't stop but made her way into the club and found Master Max by the bar. "Master Max."

He turned, and his gaze took in her clothing. "Brianna, I believe you know our rules."

Max's cold tone sent a shiver though her, but she straightened her spine and lifted her chin. "Yes, but right now I don't care about the clothing rules."

"You're upset."

"I'm mad, angry, furious." She wanted to stomp her foot, but that was going a little too far. Max glanced over her shoulder.

"Did Rafe do something?"

"No. Rafe is fine. But there is something I need to tell you, and I'd rather not have an audience doing it."

"All right. Let's go into my office."

"Could you please send one of the other subs into the women's bathroom?"

Max frowned and waved over Sierra. "Honey, would you please go check on whomever is in the bathroom."

"Of course, Sir." Sierra glanced from Brianna to Max and back.

"It's Emily," Brianna whispered into Sierra's ear.

Sierra frowned and left.

Max gestured for Brianna to follow him. Once inside his office, Brianna realized Rafe was with them. She glanced at him.

"I'm not leaving you."

Brianna nodded. It felt good to have support.

"Tell me who is in the bathroom and what the hell is

going on," Max said.

"Emily is in the bathroom, and some Dom named Ward assaulted her." Damn, she hadn't meant to blurt that out like that.

Max's eyes turned stormy, and he kept his gaze on her. "Rafe, please go get Jordan and Damon. Send Tessa and Crystal to be with Sierra and Emily."

"Will do." Rafe left.

"Sit down, Brianna. You must know I would take an accusation like this seriously."

"Yes." She sat down in the plush office chair. "I believe Emily."

He nodded. "I'll only make you tell the story once when Jordan and Damon get here."

"I appreciate that." Not that she had a complete story, but enough. Damon and Jordan walked in with concern on their faces. "Where's Rafe?"

"He stayed in the club; said he needed to watch someone," Jordan said. "What's going on?"

"Brianna, please tell us what Emily said."

Brianna took a deep breath and then repeated what Emily told her. It was short, but by the end, all the men in the room were simmering with anger.

"I thought we had him straightened out," Jordan said.

"After the incident with Kaley, I thought so too," Max said.

"What happened with Kaley?" Brianna had chatted with Kaley several times.

"Nothing major. Ward grabbed her wrist one night when she was behind the bar." Max looked at her. "Why don't you go back to Emily; we will be there shortly to make sure she's okay."

Brianna nodded. The tension in the room was thick,

and she had a feeling things were not going to go well for Ward. She made her way back into the bathroom. Sierra, Crystal, and Tessa surrounded Emily. Emily looked up at Brianna and whispered, "Thank you."

* * * *

Rafe watched Ward from the bar after Kaley pointed him out. Thankfully, she didn't ask him why he wanted to know which Dom was Ward. Hell, the man wasn't a Dom. He was a predator. Max walked in and motioned to Logan before they walked out.

A short time later, Max and Logan walked in and didn't even hesitate; they walked directly over to Ward and marched him out of the club, Rafe following.

In the lobby were two police officers plus Jordan and Damon.

"You're done," Max said to Ward.

"What is going on?" Ward asked, eyeing the police officers.

"You're under arrest," Logan said, nodding at the other two officers.

"What?" Ward struggled when the officers pulled his arms behind his back.

"You're under arrest for sexual assault. You have the right to remain silent, anything you say can and will be used against you in a court of law. You have the right to an attorney. If you can't afford one, one will be appointed to you. Do you understand these rights?" Logan asked.

"I do. And Emily is a fucking liar. That bitch."

Max took a step forward. Jordan and Damon grabbed him by the arm, and Logan glared at him.

"I never mentioned who turned you in, asshole. Take him in and book him. I'll meet you at the station with the victim's statement," Logan told the other two officers.

They nodded and marched Ward out of the club. "Sexual assault?" Rafe asked, trying to wrap his head around what just happened.

"I need to talk with Emily. I'll go put a shirt on." Logan left.

"I'll get the women out of the bathroom," Rafe said. All eyes turned to him. "I'm probably the least intimidating one of the bunch of us."

Max nodded. "All right. We're going to need someplace to talk."

"Classroom," Jordan suggested.

"I'll close the curtains and let Colby, Zeke, and Gabriel know to keep that area clear," Damon said.

"I like that. Bring the women to the classroom when they're ready. We'll wait as long as Emily needs."

Rafe blew out a breath before he stuck his head into the women's bathroom. "May I come in?"

"Yes, Rafe," Brianna's voice called out.

He moved into the room and saw the women huddled around Emily. "Hi, Emily," he said softly. "We've met before, but I don't know if you remember."

"I do. Is he—Is he gone?" Emily asked.

Rafe wasn't sure how much to tell her. "Max would like to speak with you."

"Am I in trouble?" Emily's voice was soft.

"No, you absolutely are not," Sierra said. "Logan needs to hear your story; that is all."

"Will you stay with me?" Emily asked.

"Of course, we will." All the women spoke at the same time. Sierra and Crystal held onto Emily's arms as they stood.

"Where are we going?" Sierra asked.

"Classroom."

She nodded, and Rafe followed the group of women out. He knew the subs took care of their own, but he'd not really seen it in action until now. He glanced at Brianna. "You okay?"

"Once this gets settled, I will be."

* * * *

Three hours later, the club was closed. Logan had gotten Emily's statement. Dane and Regina offered to take Emily home with them until Zeke could swing by tomorrow and put better locks on her doors and make sure a security system was installed.

A family, Brianna thought. They were like a family rallying around a member who needed help. Her heart warmed. Maybe one day she'd belong to a family like this.

"I need a drink," Jordan said, sitting next to Crystal at the group of tables and chairs they'd pulled around so everyone could sit and talk.

"Wrong place," Kaley commented.

"Not anymore," Sierra said, walking in with Max. Both of them carried bottles. Several of them.

"Out from behind the bar, Kaley. I'll take over," Max said.

"Yes, Sir." Kaley came out from behind the bar and over to Anthony. He drew her onto his lap.

"Drop the protocols, everyone," Max said, opening the first bottle. "I have red or white wine, vodka, and tequila."

Orders started flying. Brianna understood. It had been a hell of a night.

"What would you like?" Rafe asked her.

"Red, please." She didn't want anything too heavy. While she knew they wouldn't play after drinking, she also didn't want to have a hangover in the morning from heavy alcohol use.

After everyone had a drink, Brianna glanced at Max as he came to the table. "Can I ask a question?" She didn't want to offend anyone here.

"Go for it," Max replied.

"How did Ward get past all your screening?"

"Damn good question," Damon said.

"It doesn't make sense," Colby said. "We all talked with him when he grabbed Kaley, and he swore it was an accident, and he didn't mean to."

"He even apologized to me," Kaley commented.

"Plus, he went through all the classes again after Dani told us that Ward wasn't taking no from the subs when he asked them to scene, and he passed his probation period without issue." Max rubbed his forehead.

Brianna processed their words. "He was able to hide his true self so as not to alert any of you." All eyes turned her way.

"But how?" Tessa asked.

"I'm taking a guess, since I wasn't here when the incidents happened, but based on the screening process Max makes everyone go through, I wonder how Ward slipped through?" Brianna pondered her next words.

"The subs did talk though," Crystal commented.

Max's gaze zeroed in on her. "Talked how?"

"Tone it down, honey." Sierra laid her hand on his arm, and instantly Max's shoulders sagged.

"Just passing comments, nothing concrete." It was the truth.

"Damn it, we do extensive background checks, and nothing flagged," Jordan said, taking a swig of his vodka tonic.

"Did he ever mention being at another club?" Brianna's mind puzzled the pieces together. She sometimes saw things others didn't. It helped her be a better teacher.

"No," Max answered. "The BDSM community is a small one, and someone would have mentioned an issue."

"Is that really true?" Allyson piped up. "Not all clubs have rules or are SSC. The ones I used to attend in Seattle didn't. I doubt anyone would mention someone like Ward."

"Fuck," Max spit out.

More pieces, Brianna thought. "If not all clubs have rules, it could be he was going to other clubs."

"Then why join here?" Zeke asked, holding Allyson close.

"Power," Anthony muttered.

"Power, ego, whatever floated his boat," Rafe said.

"All of that is probably right," Brianna said. "He was arrogant to think he wouldn't get caught, and he escalated his need for power. I know you all know sexual assault is not for sexual satisfaction. It's for power over another."

Out of the corner of her eye, she saw Rafe stiffen. "And before anyone gets their dander up, it hasn't happened to me. I've taken a lot of psychology classes."

"But you're an elementary school teacher," Rafe said.

"I still had to understand basic human behavior."

"Well, damn," Colby muttered.

"I don't think Ward realized how close of a family you all are."

"What do we do now?" Sierra asked.

"I've already removed his code from the security system," Max said.

"Logan has Emily's side of the story," Kaley said.

"I've talked with Emily about an emergency temporary restraining order. I'll file it first thing tomorrow and make some calls," Jordan commented.

"It's the weekend, so arraignment won't be until Monday," Crystal added.

"Will he get out on bail?" Brianna asked.

"More than likely," Jordan said.

"Then we make sure Emily is safe," Sierra replied.

"She will be, honey." Max put his arm around his wife. "While the restraining order isn't foolproof, new locks, an alarm system, and all of us we'll make sure of it."

Brianna's heart swelled. This is what she missed: Being a part of something special. And these people were remarkable.

"Well, I don't know about anyone else, but I've had enough excitement for a Friday night," Colby said, standing up.

"Yeah." Zeke stood, as well. "The club is going to be open tomorrow?"

"Yes," Max said.

Everyone carried their glasses and the empty bottles to the bar. Kaley slipped behind the bar, loaded the glasses into the dishwasher, and tossed the bottles into the recycle bin.

"Kaley, you didn't need to do that," Max said.

"It's done." Kaley smiled as Anthony pulled her into his arms.

All but Max and Sierra walked out into the parking lot. Rafe helped Brianna into his vehicle, and they followed the line of cars out.

"Sorry our scene didn't happen," he said.

"It's okay. I just hope…" She sighed.

"You're worried about Emily."

"Yes. She was assaulted. No one should have to deal with that on their own."

"Brianna." Rafe reached over and picked up her hand from where it lay in her lap. "I can promise you she isn't. Regina is a nurse; she'll make sure Emily is okay and gets therapy or whatever help she needs." He squeezed her fingers. "Everyone at the club will be there for Emily."

"I want to help, but I'm not sure how."

"You already did."

"How?"

"You talked with her. You were able to get her to tell you what was bothering her, and you informed Max."

"It doesn't seem like much." It didn't to her. Maybe it was because she was used to helping kids when they scraped their knees or when they were upset. She got resolution in those instances. This… This would bother Emily for the rest of her life.

"It's a big thing, and I'm happy you were there for her."

"Thank you." Brianna tightened her fingers around his. "There's always tomorrow night."

"That there is." He lifted her hand to his lips and kissed her fingers.

All too soon, they arrived at her apartment building. Rafe insisted on escorting her to her apartment door.

"Would you allow me to check your apartment?"

Brianna looked at him. "Why?"

"One of those little protective things I like to do."

She shrugged and handed him the keys. Rafe unlocked the door and pushed it open. "Lights are on the right."

He reached over and flipped them on. "Be right back."

Shaking her head, Brianna watched as he walked through her apartment, checking windows and in the corners. She'd never had an issue, but she was coming to realize how protective these dominant men were.

Tonight showed her that. How they kept touching their subs or wives. Keeping some sort of contact in comfort and care. She sighed. She wanted that. Was that something she could have with Rafe? Too early to know. They were just starting out together.

"Everything's good."

"Thank you."

He cupped her chin. "At any time, if you feel unsafe or need me, just call me."

Her heart warmed. "I will."

"Good. I'll pick you up at seven tomorrow for the club."

"I can do that." It was Saturday, and she was looking forward to it.

"I'm going to kiss you now." He pulled her into his arms and lowered his head.

Brianna opened her mouth to his. Their tongues tangled, chasing each other around as they embraced. Oh yeah, Rafe knew how to kiss. Not sloppy or hurried. He took his time with her, and she enjoyed every second of it.

He broke the kiss, and she tried to catch her breath. "Until tomorrow." Rafe brushed another kiss over her lips before he closed the door. "Lock up."

She was still trying to figure out what he said when he maneuvered her into her apartment. "Yes, Sir."

Flipping the deadbolt and the door lock, she waited.

"'Night, my Brianna."

His words sent a shaft of longing through her. He called her "my Brianna". A warmth grew inside her, a feeling she'd never known before.

Yes, she wanted to be his.

Chapter 6

A sense of relief came over Rafe as Brianna walked out of the bathroom at the club on Saturday night. He understood last night's abrupt cancellation of their scene wasn't her fault. It wasn't anyone's fault.

Seeing her in boy shorts and a sports bra caused his cock to pulse. They were still getting to know each other. "You look delicious."

"Why, thank you, Sir. May I say you take my breath away."

Rafe glanced down. Fortunately, his cock wasn't visible, and he wasn't wearing anything different than he normally did. Leather pants, no shirt, and loafers. But her words warmed him. "Thank you." He held his hand out.

Brianna placed her hand in his, and they walked into the club together. The music was low tonight, and the club only about a quarter full. Max waved him over to the bar area.

"Evening, everyone," Rafe said as he helped Brianna onto one of the tall bar stools and stood behind her.

"I'm glad you came back," Max said.

"Why wouldn't we, Sir?" Brianna asked.

Max blinked. "Brianna, you are a breath of fresh air. This is not normal club attendance for a Saturday night."

"I don't understand." She glanced up at Rafe.

"I have a feeling people are upset about what happened last night." He placed his hands on her shoulders and pulled her against him.

"Yes." Max sighed.

"Apparently," Jordan said. "Ward had won over some of the other Doms, and they've been calling all day, upset at Ward's arrest and blaming Emily."

"That's absolute bullshit," Brianna blurted out.

Rafe's hands tightened on her shoulder as Max and Jordan stared at her.

"Sorry, Sirs. I didn't mean to speak out of turn."

"You're right," Jordan commented. "It is BS."

"While we haven't had a bad incident in years, I thought when Dani told us the subs were leery of him and we put him through the classes again, things were going to work out." Max ran his hand over the back of his neck.

"We all did," Jordan said.

"You said last night there was an incident with Kaley… Sir."

Her hesitation reminded him she was still learning. "Good girl," Rafe whispered in her ear. "For remembering protocols."

"He grabbed her arm one night. She called her safe word after he refused to let go. Ward insisted it was an accident, apologized to Kaley, and promised it would never happen again."

"That was a few months ago too," Max added. "Nothing since then."

Rafe thought about the times he'd been in the club. He had seen Ward around, but not really scening with anyone.

"Can we please stop talking about Ward," Logan commented, coming up to the group. "I've had to deal with Ellie being upset since last night." He glanced across the room where Ellie was manning the food tables.

The men all groaned. "Sorry," Max said.

"Not your fault. But I'm sick of that man's name."

"Don't blame you." Jordan clapped him on the back. "You had to deal with his arrest and everything."

"Yeah, but I don't think that's why you were talking about him. Other issues, Max?" Logan asked.

"Other Doms think Ward is innocent. I'm not sure what I can do."

"Nothing," Rafe said. He wasn't usually one to get into club business, but he needed to in this case. "Look, I'm no expert, but I've seen a lot as a firefighter. This isn't something you or anyone else can fix. It's up to the others to make a decision. Hopefully, this will blow over once the charges are upheld by the court."

"Rafe is right," Logan commented. "Arraignment is Monday. From there, the judge will set a trial date."

"Emergency restraining order is in place, and we have a court date for a permanent restraining order," Jordan said.

"Sir, has anyone talked with Emily?" Brianna asked.

"Crystal and Sierra went to see her at Regina and Dane's place today. They said she was doing okay. She wanted to go home, so they took her." Max glanced up. "Well, that answers that question."

Rafe turned his head. Regina, Dane, and Emily walked into the club together.

"Excuse me, Sir." Brianna jumped off the stool and hustled over to the group. She said something to Emily, who grinned, and the two women embraced.

Dane gave Regina a kiss and sauntered over to us.

"Everything okay?" Jordan asked.

"Fine. Emily wanted to come tonight, so we volunteered to be her ride." Dane motioned to Kaley. "Lemon-lime soda, please." He glanced at everyone. "At least I can pretend it's vodka."

Laughter rang out, and Rafe relaxed. The group would be okay. Ward might have shaken everyone up, but the family was intact. Brianna smiled at him when she hopped back up on the stool.

"Thank you, Sir," she said, when he put his hands on her waist. He glanced at her wristband. He'd talk with her about changing it, because she was no longer available to any other Dom but him.

"Max, can I get the bondage table at ten tonight?" He wanted her to know he wanted to scene with her. Not that he hadn't mentioned it.

"Sure. I have a feeling we might have a slow night," Max said.

"Then it's up to us to spice things up a bit," Dane said, pulling Regina to his side.

"Yes, let's have some fun tonight," Regina said.

"Better music coming up," Kaley said, and seconds later, techno rock came over the speakers.

"I'm on DM duty," Jordan said. "Time to get to work."

"Emily, may I escort you around the club?" Max held his arm out to her.

"Thank you, Master Max, but—"

"That's my job tonight," Noah said, coming up to all of them. "Emily and I had a long talk today."

Max nodded. "Enjoy yourselves."

Noah held his hand out to Emily, and they walked off together.

"Noah and Emily?" Max commented.

"Looks like it," Rafe said.

"It's about damn time," Kaley said. Everyone looked at her. "Hey, we work behind the bar together, and we chat."

Max shook his head. "I've been missing a lot, apparently."

"No, you haven't," Damon said, coming up to them with Tessa on his arm. "This was something out of our control."

"Damon's right," Tessa said.

"I do think we need to figure out how to prevent it from happening again," Max said.

Brianna leaned back against Rafe and tilted her head to look at him. Her eyes were filled with concern but also questions. "Go ahead, sweetheart. Speak your mind," he encouraged her.

Max looked at her, and Brianna stiffened.

"Rafe is right. What's on your mind?" Max settled on the stool next to her.

"Sir, you couldn't have prevented this. The attack didn't happen in the club. I know you feel responsible." Brianna raised her hand but didn't touch Max until he nodded.

Rafe swelled with pride. She was asking for consent.

"We can't be responsible for things that happen outside our control. Trust me. I want to protect my kids at school and at home. I've had to deal with stuff I'd hoped never to see in my career, but I also had to come to the realization that I can't control what happens when they leave my classroom. Put the blame where it belongs— with the person who committed the horrible deed."

Max stared at Brianna in silence. "Brianna, you are a treasure." Max glanced at Rafe, and he nodded. Max put his free hand over Brianna's where it laid on his arm. "Thank you for your words. Sometimes I take on burdens I don't need to."

"I tell you that all the time," Sierra commented, coming up behind Max and slipping her arms around his waist to hug him.

"I know you do."

Brianna dropped her hand.

"I still don't understand how he slipped through every safeguard we have."

Logan let out a loud sigh. "Max," he started. "The man was good at hiding what he was. A predator. Yes, he slipped up a time or two, but not enough to make us suspicious. I know you want to control everything, but you can't control others."

"Only my sub." Max grinned. "I get it. I do. It doesn't sit right with me; that's all."

"Of course it doesn't," Rafe said. Gazes turned to him. "You're like all of us. You want to protect and take care of what's yours. Sometimes we can't do that, and we blame ourselves."

Max closed his eyes and took a deep breath. "Damn right. Okay." He took another breath and let it out. "No more recriminations. Let's enjoy ourselves tonight."

Rafe glanced down at Brianna. "Let's go chat for a minute," he said softly.

She nodded. Rafe excused them from the group and took Brianna over to the quiet area. He sat down and then pulled her into his lap. Her startled gaze met his. "I want to hold you."

"Yes, Sir."

"What you said to Max was what he needed to hear. Thank you."

"I don't want him to feel bad. This isn't his fault. Ward is a predator. I've seen it before, Sir."

"In teaching?" He didn't like the thought of her being around people like that.

"Yes and in the world in general." A shiver swept over her.

He hated the idea of Brianna seeing the violent side of the world. It wasn't something he could completely protect her from, but he'd do his best.

"You're stronger for it." The words flowed out of him because he did see her strength.

"I'm glad you think so."

"You are." He squeezed her shoulders. "Let's chat about tonight. You put on your questionnaire that bondage was a soft limit."

"Yes, Sir." She shifted in his lap.

"There's a reason I asked Max for the bondage table. I also want to make sure you're comfortable going topless in the scene."

"What are you planning, Sir?"

"More sensation play, but this time, I'm going to surprise you with the items. Is a blindfold okay?" She nodded, but he caught the wary look in her eyes. "What has you concerned?"

"It's nothing."

"It's something. Talk to me."

She swallowed. "Just something from my childhood. This is a totally different situation, Sir."

There was a story there, and he'd be ready to listen whenever she was ready to tell him. "You do remember that your safe words apply, no matter what."

"Yes, Sir."

"Don't hesitate to use them. I mean that."

"I understand, Sir."

"All right. You ready?"

"Is it time?"

"Almost." He turned her so her back was against his chest, with his hands on her waist, until it was time for them to scene.

* * * *

Brianna walked with Rafe to the bondage table stage, her heart pounding. It wasn't that she didn't want to do this. She did. It was the blindfold. A shiver racked her body. Childhood fears raised their heads. Her cousin had blindfolded her for a surprise, and it wasn't something she ever wanted to experience again.

Rafe left her at the stage as he went to grab his bag from the cubbies by the bar. She took several deep breaths and let them out as her therapist told her to do when fears overwhelmed her. This was a totally different situation. She wasn't a child, and she trusted Rafe.

He took her hand and helped her up onto the stage. "I can feel you trembling," he said softly.

"I'm sorry, Sir."

Rafe dropped his bag by the small table and tugged her into his embrace. "We don't have to do this."

His eyes were filled with concern as she gazed at him.

"Rafe." Brianna lifted her hand and placed her fingers on his cheek. "It's not you or the scene."

"Then what is it?"

"As I said, a childhood fear of being blindfolded." She wasn't ready to go into a full-blown explanation. "I want to do this with you. Only you."

The concern softened. "We can skip the blindfold."

She shook her head. "I'll be fine, Sir. I know it's

you."

"All right. But I'll be watching you carefully." His palms skimmed over her shoulders before he maneuvered her around. "Still okay with going topless?" She nodded. "Arms up."

She did as he said, and he pulled her sports bra up and over her head. It was then she realized Rafe had turned her so she wasn't facing the club but the wall. He was protecting her. Her heart swelled. This man was so good to her.

"Let me help you onto the table." He captured her hand. "I'm going to start with you on your front and then turn you over."

"Yes, Sir." She hadn't addressed him properly all the time, and she would need to be careful about that. Brianna climbed onto the bondage table and laid down. Good thing she didn't have big boobs. They would have been squished as she laid down. Even now, it wasn't exactly comfortable.

She shifted as Rafe walked around the table and picked up his bag. Her head was turned in his direction, so she saw him preparing.

He pulled a set of restrains from his bag and held them up for her. "They're padded, so they won't abrade your skin."

"Okay, Sir." The fastening of the cuffs around her wrists caused her skin to tingle. She hadn't expected the weight of them. She watched as he put two double ended hooks together, then connected them to the D-ring in the restraints and the other end to the bondage table.

Brianna tugged. Oh, this was different. She couldn't see Rafe, but his fingers were warm against her ankles as he did the same with them. She was well and truly restrained. Her heart pounded. Anticipation flowed through her.

"How are you doing?"

"Green, Sir." Was she? Excitement thrummed through her. Some apprehension, too, but mostly excitement.

"All right." He pulled out a blindfold. "It's satin, so it will be soft against your face, and it has elastic bands."

"Yes, Sir." She swallowed as Rafe placed the bands over her head and slid the blindfold into place. He was right. It was soft and comfortable against her skin. He adjusted the mask.

"Can you see anything?"

"Not really. Just a little bit of light from the bottom, but that's it, Sir." That was enough to keep her fears at bay.

"Good." His touch was gone, and she took a deep breath and concentrated on what she could hear. The techno music wasn't too loud, and there weren't a lot of voices tonight, but she couldn't figure out where Rafe was. Ah, wait. He was at his bag; she heard the rustle of the leather as he removed things.

She took a deep breath and let it out. Laying here waiting ratcheted up her excitement. Something soft touched her shoulder, and she jerked in the restraints.

"Easy, sweetheart." Rafe's voice was close and soft.

"Yes, Sir." Focusing on the sensations and her breathing, Brianna relaxed against the table. It was a feather, soft and silky against her skin. Yes, it tickled at times, but it had awakened her nerves.

Then it was gone, and something different replaced it. She concentrated. This toy had multiple…tails… Is that what she was feeling? It wasn't as soft as the feather, but it wasn't hard against her body either. Her skin heated as Rafe ran it over her back, ass, and legs.

Her nipples grew hard, and her pussy tingled. She hadn't expected to get aroused so easily. The toy was removed and replaced with something hard. It didn't hurt, but it was flat and hard as he ran it over her skin.

The next toy had a sharpness to it. Almost like spikes, but they didn't dig into her skin or anything. She brought her shoulders up as Rafe teased her with it. Brianna couldn't help but wiggle her hips when he ran it over her ass.

"Like that, do you?"

"It's different, Sir." Was that her breathless voice?

"Good." The sensation was gone.

What was he planning next? "Ohh." Goosebumps broke out on her skin.

"How does it feel?" Rafe's voice was close to her ear.

"Unusual."

"Explain." He ran his hand over her stomach.

"Spiky, Sir." That was the only word she could think of. Whatever he had in his hand wasn't sharp, but did have pointed tips. Now that she was concentrating on it, she realized it was more than one point.

"You're covered in goosebumps."

"Yes, Sir. It's…" She shivered as he ran it over her spine. "Strange."

"Do you know what it is?"

"No, Sir." She swallowed. "You started with a feather; the second item had more to it, but this one, I have no idea."

"I wouldn't expect you to know." He removed his touch and cool air wafted over her.

Her skin was hot and tight. She hadn't expected to react this way. Brianna waited, but nothing happened until something frozen touched her skin. She cried out.

"That's cold, Sir."

Rafe chuckled. "Yes, it is, but your skin is so warm it's melting."

"Where did you get an ice cube, Sir?" That's what it had to be.

"The bar. I had Max bring me a glass of it."

Water trickled down her skin, and this time, she heard the ice tinkle in the glass as he picked up another piece. Brianna shivered as he ran this piece over her ass and her feet.

"So pretty," he whispered, then the ice was gone.

She waited trying to control her breathing, but it wasn't easy. Anticipation was killing her.

"Let's try this." His fingers squeezed her ass and then caressed the globes.

"Perfect," he murmured. "Let's get you turned over." The restraints were released, but she didn't want to move. Leaving it to Rafe, he gently rolled her over and redid the restraints.

He began running his hands over the front of her body, from her toes to her head and back again. Rafe stopped at her breasts, and he cupped them, rubbing her nipples with his thumb.

A moan left her lips at his touch. Soft and tender. Slowly she began to let her mind float away until…

* * * *

Rafe watched Brianna very carefully. He didn't want her to panic with the blindfold on, but she seemed fine. He was having fun, introducing her to new sensations. He used the toys on her and then the ice. Now, he caressed her breasts and nipples.

He wondered how long it would be before she realized her nipples were growing hot. After the ice, he decided to use a little bit of warming gel on her nipples. Her breathing deepened. She was getting into the zone.

"Hot," she whispered as her body stiffened.

Time to bring her back to the present. He leaned over and blew on her nipples.

"Damn." She pulled at the restraints.

"Easy, baby." Rafe grabbed the warm washcloth and bathed her nipples, removing the gel. There would still be a lingering feeling, but it should go away quickly. He'd been very careful not to use a lot of it so it wouldn't irritate her skin.

Brianna breathed out a sigh when he finished cleaning up her breasts, and she relaxed against the bondage table. Rafe removed the blindfold, then turned to drop everything back into his bag, zipped it shut, and began undoing the restraints. Damn, she was beautiful lying there, waiting for him to play with her, but that was enough for tonight.

"How are you feeling?"

"I'm fine, Sir." Her voice was soft and her body lax.

Rafe grinned. "I bet." He finished undoing the restraints, then gathered her up in a blanket and carried her to the aftercare area, settling her on the sofa. "I'll be right back. Don't move."

"Yes, Sir." She snuggled against the cushions.

Rafe cleaned up the scene and put his bag back into his cubby. Kaley was standing at the end of the bar and handed him bottled water. "Thanks."

He walked back to Brianna who still sat in the same spot, her head resting against the back of the sofa. Setting the bottle on the table, Rafe lifted her into his arms before he sat and cradled her in his lap.

"Brianna." He brushed a strand of hair away from her face.

"Hi." Her voice was soft, but when she looked at him, her eyes were clear.

"How are we doing?"

"Wonderful, Sir."

"Close your eyes and rest." He brushed a kiss over her forehead as she snuggled into his arms.

She'd done so well tonight. Her reactions were a little more than he'd been expecting and wonderful for the play they did. Rafe was happy with everything. Maybe next week they'd move up to a little more.

Chapter 7

Brianna yawned as she watched her class during lunch on Monday. She couldn't seem to wake up this morning.

"Late night?" Ruby, one of her fellow teachers, asked.

"Not really." More like erotic dreams keeping her hot and bothered.

"You need to get a life."

She didn't take offense at Ruby's words. "Not all of us can find the love of our lives." Ruby had found her soulmate a few months ago. Brianna tilted her head. Had she found hers in Rafe?

Too early to be thinking like that. They'd barely started a relationship outside of the club. Brianna grinned. Rafe had called her twice yesterday to see how she was after their scene. He was so protective and concerned.

He'd laughed when she'd told him so. Her blood heated, remembering their conversation.

"What are you thinking? You're blushing," Ruby said.

"None of your business."

Ruby laughed. The bell rang, and they ushered their

kids back into their classrooms. Brianna, feeling a little distracted, decided to let the kids do art this afternoon, since it gave her a chance to get her thoughts in order.

* * * *

Rafe stepped out of his firefighting gear and stowed it. It had been a busy week, and it was only Wednesday.

"That's the third call today," Tim said as they made their way upstairs.

"At least they've been fairly easy. Two medicals and one minor fire," Rafe commented. He was glad the calls this week had been fairly easy. No more suspicious fires, at least for now. Rafe sat on the sofa and pulled out his phone.

Brianna had been on his mind the last few days. They'd talked on Sunday but not since then. He decided to text her.

Rafe: *Hi, sweetheart, would you be interested in dinner tomorrow night? I get off at six.*

He glanced at his watch. It was almost four. Maybe she was done with her kids and could get to her phone. Damn, he was never this impatient, but he wanted to hear from her. His phone pinged.

Brianna: *Sure. Why don't you come to my place, and I'll cook. If you're too tired when you get off tomorrow, just let me know.*

Rafe: *We can go out. I don't want to make you cook.*

Brianna: *It's nothing. I'm not a fancy cook, so it will be easy. What time will you get here?*

Rafe: *Seven, if all goes well.*

Brianna: *That works for me. Text me when you leave, so I know you're on your way.*

Rafe: *Will do.*

"I see that satisfied grin. Date with a woman

tonight?" Tim teased him.

"Tomorrow." Rafe rubbed his hands on his pants. He couldn't wait to see Brianna again.

* * * *

Brianna checked the meatloaf as her phone pinged. Picking it up, she looked at the message:

Rafe: *On my way. Be there in about twenty minutes.*

Brianna: *Perfect. We can eat as soon as you get here.*

She checked the potatoes; they were cooked. Draining them, she pulled cream and butter out of the fridge and found her potato masher. She hoped Rafe like meatloaf, mashed potatoes, and roasted carrots.

* * * *

"Something smells delicious," Rafe said when Brianna opened the door.

"Dinner."

"I think it's more than dinner." He leaned over and brushed a kiss on her cheek. Brianna gestured for him to enter her apartment. He'd been here before, now he glanced around with fresh eyes.

Her sofa was across from a modest TV, a colorful blanket thrown over the back. She had two side tables with lamps and several bookcases filled with books on one wall. A small desk and chair sat against the other wall. Probably where she did her lesson plans for the kids.

"Dinner is about ready. I hope meatloaf, mashed potatoes, and roasted carrots are okay." She shut the door and leaned against it.

"It's fine. Better than me grabbing fast food on the way home."

She frowned. "That's not good for you."

Rafe couldn't help grinning. "I know, but after a

twelve-hour shift, I'm too tired to cook if I forgot to do my normal dump and go meals."

"Dump and go?" She gestured for him to sit. "Would you like something to drink?"

He stood near the sofa. "Dump and go is meal prep for the slow cooker. What do you have to drink?" Since this wasn't a play night and he didn't have to go to work tomorrow, he could indulge a little bit.

"Beer, wine, soda, water, or I can make iced tea if you'd like." A beeping noise came from the kitchen. "I need to get dinner out of the oven." She turned and disappeared through the doorway.

Rafe followed, admiring Brianna's firm ass as she bent over to take things out of the oven. *Easy, guy.* This was just a friendly dinner and maybe the start of something more.

His mouth watered as she pulled the meatloaf out. Beef and spices filled his senses. Next came a pan of roasted carrots. "That looks so good."

She jumped. "I didn't realize you followed me." Brianna reached for a platter and expertly moved the food from the pans and onto it, then she lifted the lid from a big pot that sat on the stove.

"You made mashed potatoes from scratch?" Rafe stood there, stunned. Not even his mother made mashed potatoes from scratch.

"Yes. It's not that hard."

"Damn woman, why hasn't some man snatched you up by now?" He was floored at how much trouble she went to for him. How was it he'd gotten so lucky to be paired with Brianna?

"When I say cooking was part of the problem, will you understand?" She dished up the potatoes and looked at him.

"No. Wait until I cook for you and then you'll understand your cooking is not the problem." He reached for the platter and bowl. "I'll put these on the table, and I'll take a beer to drink, please." Rafe left the kitchen. Were the men in her life crazy? Must be. He found her small table with two chairs already set. He set the food down and waited until Brianna came to the table with a tray holding his beer, a glass of wine, and a gravy boat.

Rafe held a chair out for her. Brianna's eyes widened. "Thank you," she whispered as she sat.

"You're welcome," Rafe took his place across from her and waited.

"Please, grab some food." She gestured to the food. "You're my guest."

He nodded and began to fill his plate. Everything looked delicious. He held the platter of meat and carrots out to Brianna. Rafe kept his gaze on her as she dished up her food. He enjoyed watching her expressions, the way her eyes narrowed when she concentrated on something or the quick quirk of her lips when she finished a task.

Once their plates were full, Rafe dug in. The meatloaf was rich in flavor and moist. The mashed potatoes whipped to perfection, and the carrots crunchy. "This is delicious."

Her cheeks pinked. "It's nothing."

That was the second time she put her accomplishments in the kitchen down. "It's more than nothing." He waited, but she kept her gaze lowered. "Brianna, look at me, please."

Her gaze met his. "You are a good cook. This is a meal anyone can appreciate, and if they don't, they're idiots."

Brianna shook her head. "Some men don't."

Who had made her think her cooking wasn't worthy of them? "Like I said, idiots. Don't let them define you." He didn't know how to get through to her. "Brianna, I'm not blowing smoke in your face. This is delicious. I'm enjoying it and definitely appreciate you making it."

"Some might call it too fattening." Her voice was soft.

Rafe's temper shot up. He stood and approached her. Brianna glanced up and him as he slid her chair back and pulled her to her feet. "It's healthy, not fattening. Meat, carbs, and veggies, all anyone could want."

He grasped her chin when she would have looked away. "I mean this, Brianna. Don't let some previous asshole make you think less of yourself or your abilities."

She took a deep breath and let it out. "You're right. I need to forget about them."

"You do." He guided her back onto her chair, then resumed his seat.

They finished eating in a companionable silence. When they were done, Rafe helped her clear the table until Brianna shooed him out of the kitchen as she cleaned up. Rafe laughed as he made his way into the living area.

He glanced through her bookcases. Some romance books, early education books, a couple on BDSM, and… His fingers stopped over the title *Fire Survivors*. Had someone in her life been in a fire? Or had Brianna? Having a firefighter come to class and talk was one thing, taking him on in a relationship was another.

He turned when he heard her footsteps. "I didn't think about dessert," she said.

"I don't need it." Rafe held out his hand to her, and

she placed hers in his. He guided her to the sofa. "Thank you for a wonderful dinner."

"I'm glad you liked it." She turned to face him. "I packed up some containers for you. I have more than enough for myself."

"Very thoughtful." He raised his hand and ran his finger over the soft skin of her cheek. "Are you good to scene tomorrow night?"

"Yes." Her breathing hitched for a moment, and Rafe hid his smile.

"Good. Why don't we get dinner at five, and that will give us plenty of time to chat and get to the club."

"I can do that." She put her hand over her mouth as she yawned. "I'm so sorry. It's been a long week."

"It's okay. I know you have to work tomorrow, and I'm sure the kids wear you out."

"More so this week: we've had three fire alarms go off. All false alarms, thank goodness."

"Three?" He frowned. "That shouldn't be happening. I'll stop by tomorrow and check on the system."

"You don't have to do that. The principal is sorting it out."

"I know I don't have to, but it has to be an interruption for everyone."

"It is. Not to mention a little nerve racking."

"Does me being a firefighter bother you?" This was a good place to bring this up to check in with her.

"A little bit." She shivered. "Tell me how you became a firefighter to begin with. I know little boys always think they want to be one. But growing up and actually becoming one is different."

Rafe relaxed. At least, he had her talking. "True. As a little boy, I wanted to be a firefighter. But a lot of it comes from when I was fifteen."

"What happened when you were fifteen?" Brianna shifted on the sofa, bringing her body closer to his.

"My family and I lived in an apartment building. It was an older building." He placed his arm over the back of the sofa, his fingers touching her shoulder. "A fire started somewhere in the building. It was late on Saturday night. My dad shook me awake. The room was already filling with smoke. I coughed, and my dad told me to get on the fire escape and help my two sisters."

"Oh, goodness. Didn't the smoke alarms go off?"

"They didn't."

"You must have been so scared."

"I was, but I didn't show it. I helped my sisters down the fire escape and got them away from the building, watching for my parents the whole time." A chill swept over his skin even though he was in Brianna's warm apartment.

That night was etched in his mind. The cold wind blowing, them shivering in a parking lot away from the building, the sirens, and the noise of the fire. The wood crackling and popping. He'd never forget that sound.

"They finally came out on the fire escape. We were on the fifth floor, so it wasn't that far down. I held my sisters back when they wanted to run to them."

"What took them so long?"

"They were grabbing important papers, check books, and such. I found out later that my parents kept it all in a single place."

"Why did they do that?"

Rafe remembered asking his parents why. "They understood that if the fire reached our apartment, everything would be lost. They grabbed items that couldn't be easily replaced."

She nodded. "Go on."

"We watched the firefighters fight the fire. Some people were trapped, but the men got them out."

Brianna shivered, and there was a hint of fear in her eyes. He pulled her to him, wanting her to know everything turned out fine.

"No one died, thank goodness."

"Did they find out how the fire started?"

"Another reason I took this on as a career. Someone deliberately set fire to the south stairwell. We were on the north side of the building, but there were a lot on the south side who couldn't get out through the fire escape or the stairs, who required rescue."

Another shiver hit her, and Rafe rubbed the back of her neck, grounding her.

"It shaped me into wanting to be a firefighter and an arson investigator." Might as well get it all out there now.

"Arson investigator? You don't just fight fires?" There was awe in her voice.

"Most of the time, I'm a firefighter, but when needed, I am an arson investigator. I have all my qualifications. There's not a big call for one in Pleasant Valley, but there have been times when one is needed."

"I'm sure it's less dangerous."

"There are still some dangers, but I like being a firefighter."

Brianna tilted her head. "There's something in your voice; I can't put my finger on it. It's almost like…a deep respect for your profession."

He nodded. "Yes. You have to respect fire and learn how it works. It takes a lot to be a firefighter, and I respect the hell out of my colleagues."

"No, thank you. That would not be for me."

"Not everyone likes working with fire, and that's okay." When she yawned again, Rafe decided it was time to put an end to their evening. "I want you to think about our scene tomorrow night. I'm thinking some bondage and light spanking and flogging."

She was silent for a moment. "Okay."

Rafe stood, and she followed suit. "Let me get your food." She rushed off to the kitchen. He didn't want to push tonight, but at least he'd seen a bit more of Brianna's aversion to fire. It seemed to run deep. She didn't seem to mind him fighting fires, but she'd worry. He wished he could spare her that worry, but there was no way to do that. Maybe he'd talk with Logan and find out how Ellie dealt with him being a cop. Logan's odds of being hurt on the job were probably about the same as his.

Brianna came back with a small bag and handed it to him.

"Thank you." He pulled open her door. "Until tomorrow." Rafe brushed his lips over hers, then stepped outside. "Lock up."

"Yes, Sir." Her voice was soft, but that sir went straight to his cock.

"Tomorrow." Unable to resist, he kissed her again before straightening and letting her close the door. Rafe made his way to his vehicle with a big grin on his face.

* * * *

Brianna leaned against the wooden front door, trying to catch her breath. Not so much from Rafe's kiss, but from what she'd learned. He was a fire survivor. He respected fire. A shiver racked her body. How were they even compatible?

She had a healthy fear of fire from her childhood and… What? It wasn't like she was going to be involved in fire. This was Rafe's job, and yes, she'd worry about him, but just like she worried about Logan and his job, for Ellie's sake.

With a shake of her head, she checked the kitchen to make sure everything was off, then turned off the lights. In her bedroom, she got ready for bed, but she laid there awake for a long time.

She'd call Ellie on her lunch break tomorrow and see if she had time on Sunday to chat. Brianna needed to know if Ellie had any tips or tricks for dealing with Logan's job that Brianna could use.

A beep sounded. Brianna sat up. Fire alarm? Smoke alarm? She climbed out of bed, but didn't hear the beep again. Not that it mattered. She checked all the smoke alarms in her apartment, and the lights were green. She wasn't going to sleep anytime soon. Curling up on the sofa, she pulled the blanket over her, listening. Fire could happen at any time, and she would be alert for it. Never again would she let down her guard.

* * * *

Rafe sat at the desk in the small alcove of his home and finished reading the latest fire report. Suspicious, but no obvious evidence of arson. He tossed the file aside. Something about it bugged him. These fires were too coincidental. Four of them. All seemingly accidental, but something nagged him. Rafe pushed away from his desk. Time to go for a run. Otherwise, he'd sit there, going over and over the same facts and not coming to a conclusion.

After putting on his running shoes, Rafe grabbed his phone and keys. Outside his front door, he did a few stretches and then started off at a light jog until he'd warmed up enough to run. He thought back to last night.

Brianna's reaction to his story made his suspicion that her fear of fire was real. She hadn't come out and said so, but it was there. Her wide eyes, the way her body trembled, and her shallow breathing all added up to fear.

He hadn't pushed because it was getting late, and she had to work. He wouldn't dismiss her concerns that his job was dangerous. It could be, but he took precautions like everyone else.

He hoped she understood that from their chat last night. He'd need to reassure her of that to lessen her worry. His phone rang, and he stopped running for a moment. "Hello."

"Hey, Rafe, it's Max. Did I catch you at a bad time? You sound out of breath."

"Just taking a run. What's up?"

"Zeke and Gabriel just finished framing the room for fire play, and I wanted you to come by tonight before we opened to look at it."

"That was fast." They'd only talked about it a couple weeks ago.

"Yes. I wanted to get it done since attendance at the club is down." The frustration in Max's voice was evident.

"From the Ward incident."

"Yeah. I'm having all new background checks run on everyone in the club and sending out a blast email, telling everyone that the club has no tolerance for non-consent or illegal activities."

"You think that will fix the problem?"

"There are always going to be those who think Ward is innocent. But he's not in my book. I trust the subs, and the only one who ever lied to me was thrown out."

"Before my time."

"It was when I first met Sierra. I'm wondering what other precautions I need to put in place."

Rafe began walking to cool down. "Max, you do a hell of a job weeding out those who don't belong. And the subs know, thanks to your training efforts, to report any issues."

"Then why do I feel I need to do more."

"Because you're a Dom, through and through." Rafe wasn't sure what else he could say. "Ward played you and the others."

"True."

"I think re-running the background checks will give you peace of mind. You have the cameras on the property and in reception, right?"

"I can't put them inside the club. It would be an invasion of privacy. Besides, I don't keep any security video beyond a week."

Rafe stopped at the front of his house, climbed the stairs, and sat in one of the chairs he kept on the front porch. "No reason to. You keep those mainly to check who is coming to the club, along with the gate codes, and in reception to make sure nothing happens out there. You've done everything you can. Why are you doubting yourself?"

Max's sigh was loud. "I blame myself."

"Of course you do. And you can bet most every Dom who's interacted with Ward is too. But from what I saw, Emily is doing okay, and Noah is very protective of her."

"I noticed that too."

"And I bet if you talk to Noah, he's blaming himself, as well."

"He shouldn't."

"Neither should you."

"So Sierra keeps telling me."

"Listen to your wife." Rafe grinned. "Brianna and I are going to dinner before the club. Is seven-thirty enough time to check out the room."

"That's fine. They haven't done the insulation yet, just the frame. Since both of them will be at the club tonight, I'll see if they can come early. I believe they wanted to chat with you about the insulation."

"Works for me. I'll see you later." Rafe hung up and sat on his porch for a few minutes. Max took a lot on. Rafe understood Max feeling responsible, but the only one responsible for what had happened was Ward.

Surging to his feet, Rafe went inside to shower. He had a scene to plan out in his head.

* * * *

Rafe escorted Brianna from the reception area that night. "Meet you inside the club." He'd explained to her over dinner he needed to meet with Max.

"Okay." Brianna smiled at him before disappearing into the ladies' room.

Rafe changed and then walked into the club. There were only a few people here. He saw Max, Zeke, and Gabriel by the curtained off area that led to the classroom and walked over to them.

"Evening," Rafe said.

"Thanks for coming early," Max said.

"We appreciate it," Zeke said.

"I'll admit I'm anxious to see how it's coming along," Rafe commented.

"Let's go." Max held the curtain back, and the men entered.

Rafe was surprised to see how much smaller the

classroom area was. "Did you increase the dimensions?"

"I did," Max said. "We don't need a big classroom space anymore, and I'd rather we had more space than less for your work."

Rafe nodded and examined the room.

"We used all class-A plywood as you requested," Zeke said.

"Perfect." Rafe ran his finger over the wood.

"I know we talked about the insulation and flooring," Gabriel said. "But I found several types and wanted your input."

"Mineral wool would be the best for the insulation. It's pretty much fire proof."

"That was on my list, so that's what we'll use."

"Also, we'll use wood over the insulation same as the framing. What do you want for the floor?"

"Vinyl flooring is the best." Rafe was impressed with the work Zeke and Gabriel had done. "It's the highest rated. Not completely fireproof, but it's one that helps stop the fire from spreading."

"Perfect," Zeke said.

"How do you see this working out, Rafe?" Max asked. "Where would you put your equipment."

"Good question." Rafe walked around the room to get an idea. "I'll use two metal tables for the equipment. The table that I work on will be metal, but I'll provide a cushion so it's not so hard on the body."

"I can purchase everything you need," Max said.

"I already have the cushion from other demos I've given at private parties." He hadn't done a private party in a while.

"All right. I'll need the dimensions of the tables you want. Do you want a cabinet to store your supplies in?"

"That would be nice." It would save him time in having to lug his supplies and equipment around.

"I'll order a metal one, as well, since we're trying to keep everything fire resistant as much as possible."

Rafe nodded. "This is wonderful. I can't thank you enough for this." He was blown away by what Max was willing to pay for.

"We're all looking forward to it," Zeke said.

"I've always been interested in fire play," Gabriel said.

"I'm glad I could do it." Max patted Rafe on the shoulder. "Now let's go find our subs and have some fun tonight."

"Oh yes. You did put me down for the St. Andrew's cross, right?" Rafe asked as they made their way into the club.

"At nine," Max confirmed.

"Great." Rafe froze, his senses going into high alert. He glanced at the door to the club at the same time as the others did. A group of men stood there. Doms who had talked with Max about not being happy about the situation with Ward and hadn't been at the club in the last week or so.

"Excuse me," Max said and moved away.

"Hell no," Zeke said, following Max. Rafe and Gabriel followed. By the time they arrived, Noah, Damon, Dane, and Oliver had joined them.

"Master Max." Rafe wasn't sure of this man's name, but he seemed to be taking the lead.

"Alexander."

The crowded shifted. Rafe glanced toward the bar. Kaley was behind the bar, and several of the women were seated. All watching, including Emily.

"We wanted to clear the air," Alexander said.

Max nodded.

Alexander shifted from one foot to the other. "We spoke to you without knowing the full story. I apologize for that."

"So do we," the men behind him chorused.

"Ward had a hearing yesterday, and we found out this wasn't the first accusation."

Shock went through Rafe's body. Max had said the background check came in clean. How could this have slipped through the cracks?

"The prosecution showed evidence of other assaults that were swept under the rug. We won't let this one be swept away." Alexander glanced over at the bar. "Emily will be safe, and Ward is now known in the community as a predator. He will not be welcome by anyone in the lifestyle who conforms to safe, sane, and consensual as we do."

More affirmations from the men behind him echoed in the club.

"I also want to you to know, Master Max, that we agree with your rules and your leadership. This was not your fault. Ward had us all fooled, and we don't take that lightly."

Max nodded.

"I, for one, appreciate the apology." Emily's voice was loud and clear as she joined them. Noah moved to her side. Heads turned toward her, and she raised her chin. "I've played with a few of you, and you've always been kind and courteous. You never violated my hard limits or my consent."

"I am humbled by your words," Alexander said before he looked at Max. "Are we allowed back into

Wicked Sanctuary?"

"You were never banned. I only cautioned you about the rules."

A sigh of relief went up from the men. "Ms. Emily, are you okay with us being here?"

A smile lit up Emily's face. "Yes. I'm sure others will enjoy scening with you. But I'm off the market." Emily slid her arm through Noah's.

"About time," Kaley yelled from behind the bar.

Laughter filled the air. "All right, everyone, let's enjoy our evening," Max said.

The crowd dispersed, and Rafe snagged Brianna around the waist. "You stayed at the bar."

"I was warned to let you men handle it." Brianna gazed at Kaley before looking at him.

"Good call," Rafe said to Kaley.

"What were you, Max, Zeke, and Gabriel talking about?" Brianna asked.

"I hope it was about the new fire play area," Sierra jumped into the conversation.

If Rafe hadn't been watching Brianna so closely, he wouldn't have seen the flash of fear in her eyes before she masked it.

"Fire play?" Her voice was soft and had a slight tremble to it. "I thought that was off limits in the club?"

"It was," Max answered. "Several of the club members have been asking for it after Rafe did a demo of fire play in Seattle."

"They saw me in Seattle?" Rafe hadn't known that. He'd done that demo several months ago.

Max nodded. "With so many requests, we're building a special area just for fire play."

"You do fire play?" The shock in her voice was

surprising. She'd read his questionnaire.

"I do." He pulled her close as her body trembled. "I know it's a hard limit for you, and that's fine. Like Max said, it's mainly for demo purposes. If anyone wants to learn, I'll send them to the man I learned from." He didn't feel proficient enough to teach even if his mentor told him he could. "Are you okay?" Rafe whispered in Brianna's ear as the others continued to talk.

"I…" She broke away from him with her hand over her mouth and ran out of the club.

Rafe stood there. There was definitely something about fire that upset Brianna. He took a step, and Sierra stepped in front of him.

"Let me go check on her," Sierra said.

No. Brianna was his, and he needed to be the one to soothe her, to figure out what had triggered her leaving.

Max put a hand on his shoulder. "Let Sierra try first."

He nodded and watched Sierra leave the club. Rafe's gut churned.

* * * *

Brianna was glad the ladies' room was empty when she raced in like a mad woman. Fire play. It shouldn't have hit her so hard. She was perfectly aware Rafe was a Dom who did fire play. A shudder racked her body as tears gathered in her eyes. She couldn't do this. She sat on the bench and buried her face in her hands.

"Brianna, honey." Sierra's arm went around her shoulders.

"I'll be okay," she whispered, but would she?

"Why does fire play scare you so much?"

Brianna lifted her head to stare at Sierra. "I didn't say it did."

Sierra shook her head. "Your actions did. It's okay if it does, but you need to talk with Rafe about those fears."

"How can I? It's his specialty, isn't it? How can I tell him I'm afraid of something he loves to do?" Brianna wiped at her cheeks.

Sierra stood and grabbed a box of tissues and brought them over.

"You didn't see his face when you ran. The man was gutted, full of concern. For you."

Brianna took a couple of tissues. "I didn't mean to hurt him." That was the last thing she wanted, but how could she do anything different? There was no way she could be around fire play. Another shiver slid up her spine.

"Of course you didn't." Sierra patted her shoulder. "Brianna, he needs to understand."

"I…" Brianna blew her nose. Sierra was right; she owed it to Rafe to tell him about her fear. She'd been doing so well until tonight. "Give me a few minutes and tell Rafe I'll be back in the club."

Sierra nodded, hugged Brianna one more time, and left, glancing back from the door with an encouraging smile. Brianna cleaned up her face and splashed some water on her cheeks. At least she wasn't wearing mascara, or she'd look like a racoon. It was bad enough her eyes were bloodshot.

Not much she could do about that. Throwing the used tissues away and putting the tissue box back where it belonged, she stood tall as she walked from the bathroom into the club.

Rafe was waiting right inside the door. He took her hand and lifted it to his lips. "I'm sorry."

Her heart melted. He was apologizing for something

he didn't even do. This man got beneath her defenses at every turn, and she instinctually knew he had her best interests at heart. She owed him an explanation. "Can we talk?"

Rafe nodded and led her to the quiet area. Before she could sit, he sat and pulled her into his lap. "I need to keep you close."

His voice was soft, but his eyes held concern, and Brianna's own needs went out the window. "I didn't mean to hurt you." The words tumbled out of her mouth. "I'm scared, and I ran because of it."

"Sweetheart." He rubbed her back in a soothing manner. "I promise, you don't have to do fire play. I know it's a hard limit."

"It's more than that." She swallowed. Rafe was being so kind, so gentle. "I'm afraid of fire."

He blinked at her, and then his eyes widened. "I'm a firefighter."

"Yes." Her tummy tumbled over and over. "I understand your job and your need to do that job. I think I can be okay with that, as long as I don't have to watch you doing your job."

"But fire play?"

"I don't think I can watch." She twisted her fingers together in her lap. "I'm doing a crappy job of explaining this."

"How about you tell me what scares you about fire?"

"Everything." She gave a little laugh. "I have an electric stove because I can't stand the thought of an open flame."

He nodded.

"You told me the other night about how, after an apartment fire, you wanted to understand more about fire."

"Yes."

"Well, I had the opposite reaction." Her breath hiccupped in her chest. Even now, she could feel the heat from the flames on her skin.

"Will you tell me?" He shifted, keeping her body close to his.

"Is this really the place?" They were in the club, after all.

"No one will bother us, and I want you to feel safe. You feel safe here, right?"

"I feel safe with you." It was the truth. Rafe made her feel safe and cherished. They hadn't known each other that long, but she trusted her instincts.

"I'm humbled by your words."

She took a deep breath and laid against Rafe, tucking her head into the crook of his neck. She needed his grounding touch to tell this story. "When I was twelve, we had relatives visiting. I was in my room, playing with my cousin who'd always been a bit of a bully. He had a box of matches."

"Something a child should never have."

"Right. I told him to put them away, but he wouldn't listen to me. He kept striking them and then blowing them out. I was scared, but I couldn't leave. Couldn't go tell my mother. He was between me and my bedroom door."

"Why didn't you call out for help?"

"He told me if I did, he'd burn me." Her body trembled with the memories. "I thought about yelling anyway, and then he dropped a lit match. The carpet caught fire."

Rafe's arms tightened around her, and Brianna

closed her eyes, shaking as she continued. Now that she'd started, she had to get this out.

"I'm not sure why I did what I did. I was out of my mind. Instead of running out of the room, I screamed, raced for the closet, and hid."

"Brianna, open your eyes." Rafe's voice was low and commanding.

She opened her eyes to stare into the concern and fury in his. "What happened to the cousin?"

"I saw him run out of the room before I closed the door. I kept screaming, but no one heard me. My parents had no idea I was still inside until everyone gathered outside the house."

"Oh, sweetheart. How terrified you must have been."

"Beyond terrified. I was lucky, at least I think I was." She placed her palm against his cheek. "A firefighter rescued me."

"Is that why my job doesn't scare you?"

"You're so brave, going into the flames to get people out and make sure fires don't spread." She truly believed that. Brianna wasn't afraid of his job. Never was.

Rafe grinned. "So the firefighter got you out?"

"Yes. I felt so alone in that closet, but he was so strong and brave." Her features softened. "He opened the closet door, picked me up, and cradled me in his arms. He kept telling me not to be afraid, but I saw the flames licking at the bedroom door. I could feel the heat, and I was sure we were both going to die."

"But you didn't."

"No. Luckily, my bedroom was on the first floor, and the window was open, but it was too small. He had to break it out and slid me out. I was crying hysterically by then. He was so calm." After she recovered from the incident, she asked her mother to help her bake cookies for the firefighters.

Her mother had been happy to help her. She'd baked sugar cookies in the shape of fire trucks and firefighters. When they arrived at the fire station, she took a special one she'd done to the firefighter who saved her.

It was one where the firefighter carried a small child in his arms. Brianna hugged the man and thanked him for saving her. He smiled and told her that it was his job.

"That's how we are."

"I know." She placed her palm on his cheek. "No one could figure out how the fire started, and my cousin told me if I said anything, he'd make sure I didn't survive the next fire."

Rafe's arms tightened around her, and there was anger in his features.

"I know. He was a bully. But they did an investigation and found the box of matches in his pocket."

"What did they do?"

"Not much. He was a juvenile, and his parents swore up and down that he knew better than to play with matches."

"Doesn't mean a thing."

"It didn't. My parents knew I wouldn't have had access to matches. But there was no real proof who started the fire."

"You knew."

She nodded. "I want you to understand; I was scared to say anything, not for myself, but for my family. What if I said something and he came back. started a revenge fire, and everyone died? I couldn't tell anyone."

"That's a heavy secret for a child."

"That's what my therapist told me." She might as well tell him everything. "I was in therapy for years as a kid and later as an adult."

"Did it help?"

"Yes and…" She glanced away. "My cousin died when I was nineteen, and I felt guilty that I was relieved." Rafe placed a soft kiss on her temple. That little touch gave her the courage to go on. "I didn't know the rest of it until after he died. He'd been causing fires for years, but the last one, he made a mistake and got caught in the flames and died."

"I'd like to say I'm sorry, but I'm not. He was evil."

"I have to agree. I think that's why the guilt hit me. I was glad he was dead, but also wondered, if I'd spoken up before, would he still be alive?"

"Honey, don't do that to yourself." Rafe cupped her chin and tilted her head back. "He wasn't going to change, no matter what. I've seen that type of psychological disorder up close."

"I know." She tried to smile to show Rafe she was all right but couldn't quite do it. "So that's the story of why I can't be anywhere near fire."

"I understand. Now, I want you to get something through your head. Fire play is my thing. It doesn't have to be your thing. It's not something I need to do with you."

"But I thought…" His fingers covered her lips.

"I do it because I enjoy watching how fire works and how others enjoy the feeling of fire cupping."

"Fire cupping? I've heard that term somewhere." She couldn't remember where.

"Probably if you watched the Olympics. Several athletes use it to help with strained or tired muscles."

"But wouldn't it need to be done by a medical professional?"

"It can be. I want to assure you I've been fully trained. My mentor has performed fire play for over forty years. I only do fire cupping because that helps people relax the most."

Brianna relaxed against Rafe. "I'm glad you can help people with it. I just… I still don't think I can ever be around it."

"Again, you don't have to do fire play for us to be together. However, if you want to understand better, I can show you some videos. That way, you won't be so scared. This is something I enjoy, not something we have to do together."

"I think I understand." She did. Sierra had been right to nudge her to talk about her phobia. Rafe understood and didn't put her down. While her parents had gotten her therapy, they'd never understood her fear nor had any of her boyfriends.

"Good. Are you okay to scene tonight?"

"Oh my goodness, I totally forgot. Did we miss our scene time?" She knew Max kept a solid schedule.

"I had Max move us when you ran out."

Brianna kissed Rafe. "You are a wonderful man, you know that?"

"I'm glad you think so."

"I do. And yes, I want to scene with you tonight. I want to forget and let my emotions go."

"That I can do." He took her mouth in a hard passionate kiss. "For now, let's just sit here and make out like teenagers."

And they did.

Chapter 8

At ten, Rafe led Brianna over to their scene area. The conversation with Brianna still played over and over in his mind. She was a stronger woman than she gave herself credit for, and he admired her for that.

He enjoyed fire play and continued to learn about fire. Fire cupping fascinated him, and he liked how it helped people. He wished Brianna would let him show her. Maybe in time, she could watch a demo. For now, he needed to take it slow. It had to be Brianna's choice. Rafe pushed the thoughts of fire play away as he led Brianna up to their scene.

Rafe glanced at her. Her eyes were a little wide, but her body was relaxed. "Are we still green?"

"Yes, Sir." Her voice was soft but strong.

"All right." He set his bag on the table, opened it, and grabbed the restraints. "I'm going to restrain your arms and legs tonight."

"Yes, Sir." Brianna shifted from one foot to the other.

"You're saying yes, but your body language is hesitant." He didn't want her to be afraid.

Her eyes widened. "I'm sorry, Sir."

Rafe set the cuffs on the chair and walked over to Brianna. "There is no reason to be sorry. Talk to me.

What is making you hesitate?"

"Ummm." She glanced away. "You mentioned me being naked, Sir."

"Yes, clothing can get in the way of you feeling the flogger. If it bothers you, you don't have to take your bra off." He could work around it.

"I want to feel the flogger, Sir. It's…" Her gaze met his. "Can we take it off at the last minute?"

It hit him. She was still shy. "Yes, we can."

"And my boy shorts, Sir?"

"What do you have on underneath them?" Why hadn't he thought about this before tonight? Was he pushing her too fast?

"A thong, Sir."

His dick twitched at her answer. "Will you be comfortable with just the thong on?"

"Yes, Sir." Her eyes brightened.

"All right, here's what we'll do. Before I restrain your right hand, you can slip your arm out of your bra strap, then do the same with the left. Then before I restrain your legs, I'll remove your boy shorts, but leave the thong. The last thing I'll do is unhook your bra. Does that work for you, sweetheart?"

"Oh, yes, Sir." Her breathing was irregular. "Thank you."

"Brianna." Rafe framed her face with his hands. "I will always take your concerns into consideration. Never be afraid to voice them."

She grinned. "Yes, Sir."

"Now go over to the St. Andrew's cross." When she turned, he slapped her ass.

"Ohh." Brianna jumped and glanced over her shoulder at him but continued to make her way to the cross.

Rafe picked up the restrains and followed her. Within minutes, she was semi-nude and restrained. He ran his hands over her shoulders and back, then cupped her ass cheeks. "Beautiful," he whispered. Her skin flushed. "Now, my beauty, remember your voice. I want to hear you."

"Yes, Sir."

Running his fingers over her spine, Rafe walked over to his bag and pulled out a feather duster, rabbit flogger, a flogger that had fur on one side of the tails and leather on the other, and a padded wooden paddle.

He carried them over and set them on the small table next to the cross. Rafe thought about blindfolding Brianna, but he wanted to see her eyes. "I'm going to start simple with the feather duster."

"Yes, Sir."

Rafe noticed Brianna had turned her head away from the club and that was okay. They hadn't gathered a crowd yet. They probably would by the end. He twirled the feather duster over the skin of her shoulders, down her spine, across her ass, then over her legs.

Gooseflesh dotted her skin as he used the duster on her. Rafe made several passes, noting how her body rested against the cross. She was relaxing well. He took the duster away and grabbed the rabbit flogger.

He ran it over her left arm. "Soft," she whispered.

"Rabbit flogger." He continued to drag the tails over her skin. When he reached her ass, he gave her a spank.

Brianna let out a yelp, but her body relaxed right back down after his smack. He did it again and again as he ran the flogger over her skin. Then he rubbed her ass. "How are you doing?"

"Green, Sir."

He nodded, even though she couldn't see him, and brought down the rabbit flogger on the top of her thighs, then her ass, before rubbing his hand over the spots. She flushed as he continued to use the flogger over her warming skin. She didn't panic or yell. Oh, there was the occasional cry of surprise, but nothing he didn't expect.

"How are you doing, sweetheart?" He caressed her back as he spoke to her.

"Hot, Sir."

"Does that mean red?"

"No, Sir. I'm still green. My body in on fire and wants more."

Rafe leaned over. "Open your eyes, please." She did, and Rafe gazed into her clear hazel eyes. "How are your arms and legs?" He didn't want her going numb.

"Fine, Sir." She wiggled her fingers at him.

"All right, are you ready for what I plan next?"

"Oh, yes, Sir."

The eagerness in her voice made him chuckle. Putting away the rabbit flogger, he picked up the padded wooden paddle.

* * * *

Brianna began breathing through her mouth. The sensations running through her body almost overwhelmed her, and she had no idea what Rafe was planning next. The feather duster had tickled her skin and relaxed her.

The rabbit flogger, along with his spanking, awoke every nerve ending and caused her body to heat. She was hot, scorching hot. Now, she waited for his next toy. Something soft but with a hint of hardness to it ran over her shoulders and down her back.

"Ahhh," she cried out as Rafe smacked her right ass

cheek, then her left. Damn, that stung, but as he rubbed his hand over the area, heat flowed into her blood stream. Who knew something like this could be so sensual? So arousing?

Oh yes, she was aroused. Her nipples were hard little points, and her pussy clenched with every smack of…a paddle, that's what it was. It must have padding on one side. As Rafe paddled her butt and upper thighs, she began to float. This was nice. Her body was becoming light, and her muscles turned to mush.

"Brianna." Rafe calling her name seemed to come from a long way away.

Something was draped over her shoulders as Rafe undid her arm restraints. He guided her arms to her sides. Why did her arms feel so heavy?

"I've got you, sweetheart." His hands were at her waist, his leg between hers. The leg restraints were removed. Who took those off? She didn't have time to find out as she was lifted into Rafe's arms and another blanket thrown over her.

Resting her head against his shoulder, she kept her eyes closed. Her body felt so good, so relaxed, and her mind was blank.

"I'll clean up for you," a male voice commented.

"Thanks." Her body swayed as Rafe walked, then sat with her in his lap. She laid curled up in his arms. This felt so good. She loved being held by Rafe. He did things to her body she'd never let anyone else do.

And at this moment in time, she was happy they were together. There was nothing that could tear them apart. It almost sounded to her like she was in love, but that wasn't possible. They barely knew each other. But she felt so good right now, like nothing bad could ever touch her.

* * * *

Rafe cradled Brianna in his lap. "Brianna, sweetheart." He waited. Her eyes stayed shut, but she cuddled closer to him.

"Tired." Her voice was soft. Rafe breathed out a sigh of relief at her response. She'd gone into subspace. He hadn't expected it, but he noticed when her body went completely lax in the restraints. Rafe had motioned Damon over to help him release her.

He could have released her feet and held her up, but he didn't want her hanging by her wrists and possibly hurting herself. So, instead, he released her arms first, then had Damon release her ankles.

She'd collapsed into his arms. Making sure she was covered before they left the scene, Rafe tried talking to her, but there had been no response. He wasn't worried. Her breathing was good, and her skin flushed.

Once in the aftercare area, he talked to her again. She responded with a strong voice. He'd played with some of more experienced subs at Wicked Sanctuary, but none of them had gone into subspace like Brianna had.

Was it because she was new? He didn't think so. She trusted him to take her to new heights and to care for her. His heart pounded. Her trust wasn't something he'd ever violate. He sat there holding her, knowing she had captured a piece of his heart.

While that didn't surprise him, they hadn't known each other long. There was something about Brianna, even on the first day at the elementary school, that told him she was the woman for him.

Rafe shook his head. He wasn't one to believe in love at first sight, but he couldn't deny the attraction. It grew each time he saw her. Now, his heart was involved.

"Everything okay?" Max asked as he walked up to them.

"It's all good. She went into subspace."

"It might take her a bit to come out of it," Max said.

"I suspect it might." He looked around the club. There were still people there, but a lot fewer than earlier. "Closing early?"

"Maybe." Max rubbed his chin. "Damon put your bag back in the cubby."

"Thanks. Let me know if we need to leave."

Max nodded and walked away.

"Rafe." Brianna's voice was soft. He glanced down at her.

"Welcome back, sweetheart."

"I feel so…relaxed. That's the only word I can think of."

Her lashes rose. Her hazel eyes were languid, much as her body was. "I'm glad. Anything hurt?" Rafe raised his hand and ran his fingers over her cheek.

Brianna shook her head.

"Good. Just lay here until you feel like moving."

"What time is it?"

"Don't worry about it. Close your eyes and rest."

"Yes, Sir." She closed her eyes, snuggled close to him once again, and settled down.

Rafe tightened his arms around her and shifted into a more comfortable position. Tonight had changed things between him and Brianna. It was a good change. They'd work through the fire thing. Because he didn't think he'd be able to let her go now.

Chapter 9

"What time is it?" Brianna's sleepy voice jerked Rafe awake.

What the hell? He'd fallen asleep, in the club no less. That had never happened before. "I'm not sure." He glanced around the club. Several couples milled around, and a few were in scenes.

"Hey, Zeke," Rafe called, seeing him. "What time is it?"

"Almost two."

"Thanks."

"Two?" Brianna sat up in his arms.

"Easy, sweetheart." Rafe made sure the blanket stayed over her chest. "We both fell asleep."

"The last thing I remember was floating on a fluffy cloud and you holding me."

"You went into subspace. Ready to go home?"

"Yes, please." She started to scoot off his lap, but Rafe stopped her.

"Let me help you." He stood with her in his arms, then set her on her feet. She swayed for a moment.

"Whoa." She gripped his forearms.

"Dizzy?"

"A little, but it's gone now."

"Okay, let me secure the blanket around you."

"What?" She glanced down. "I'm naked." Her voice rose.

"You still have your thong on. Remember?"

She blinked. "Yes, it's starting to come back." Her cheeks turned pink.

Rafe secured the blanket around her and removed the second one. It was a good thing Max had large blankets.

"Okay, let's grab my bag, then we'll get changed."

Keeping his arm around her waist, he guided her to the bar area. "Sit here." He ushered her onto the stool before he dropped the blanket in the hamper and grabbed his bag. When he returned, she was almost falling off the stool.

"I got you." He scooped her up.

"I don't know why I'm so weak."

"You're not weak; you're just extremely relaxed. It's part of going into subspace. It's going to take a while to wear off," Kaley said from behind the bar.

Brianna glanced at her. "But I went to sleep."

Kaley grinned. "Your body is still coping with all the endorphins. Trust me. It will take a while." Kaley looked at him. "Get Max to override the locker and get her things. I can watch her while you change."

"Thanks, Kaley." He'd wondered how he was going to get Brianna dressed. "Brianna, stay here with Kaley."

"Okay." This time, he steered her to one of the sofas. It took him a minute to find Max in his office and get Brianna's things out of her locker. It only took him a couple of minutes to get ready; all he had to do was pull on a shirt and grab his wallet and keys.

"Max, is it okay if I take the blanket Brianna is wrapped in with me? I'll wash it and bring it back."

"Of course." Max waved his arm.

"Thanks." Rafe ran out to his vehicle and dropped his bag and Brianna's inside, before returning to the club and picking Brianna up in his arms. "Have a good night, Kaley."

Carrying Brianna to his SUV, he placed her in the passenger seat and fastened her seatbelt, before closing the door and getting into the driver's seat. "How are you doing?"

"I'm okay, it's just…" Her stomach growled. "I'm so sorry."

"It's fine. How about I stop and grab some fast food on the way to my house." Usually he wouldn't eat this late at night, but he was hungry too. The scene had taken energy reserves out of both of them.

"That would be nice."

Rafe pulled out of the parking lot and drove down the main road. He turned the heater on low so Brianna wouldn't get cold.

"Wait a second," Brianna said.

"Yes." He glanced at her before returning his attention to the road. Not that there was traffic, but at this time of night, deer or other animals might be out and on the road.

"You said your house."

"Yes."

"You're not taking me home?"

"Sweetheart, you're not in any shape to be alone tonight, so you're coming home with me."

"Bossy," she muttered.

"In this case, yes."

She sighed, and he couldn't suppress a grin. Once they made it to the city limits, he found an open fast-food joint, ordered them both some food, and then drove home. Brianna had been very quiet; she didn't even say anything when he ordered a burger, fries, and a shake for each of them.

Rafe pulled into the garage and turned off the engine. "Stay here," he said before climbing out. He grabbed their bags out of the back and then the food and drinks and made his way inside.

After setting the food on the counter, he dropped their bags in his bedroom, put a few things out in the bathroom, and went back to the garage. He picked Brianna up.

"You don't have to carry me," she said.

"You don't have shoes on."

"I don't." She lifted her legs and looked at her feet. "Where are my shoes?"

"You took them off before our scene." He stopped at the doorway to the house and closed the door leading to the garage. Once inside, he placed her on the sofa and went to get their food.

He plated their burgers and fries, then poured the milkshakes into glasses. He carried everything into the family room where Brianna sat.

"I'm in a blanket."

"That you are." Rafe sat the food in her lap and put their shakes on the table. "You didn't say much when I ordered food, so you can have the chocolate or vanilla shake, whichever you choose."

"Why am I in a blanket?"

Rafe frowned. "Brianna, what day is it?" He was beginning to get worried.

"Friday, well, Saturday now since it's after midnight."

"Good. Tell me what you remember about tonight."

"We had dinner, went to the club, scened, I went into subspace, you carried me to your SUV, grabbed some food, and brought me to your house."

His worry began to clear. "Right, now why do you think you're in a blanket?"

"Because…" She bit her lip, and her face flamed. "I'm semi-nude." He blew out a breath. "Sorry, I forgot for a minute." She picked up a fry and popped it into her mouth. "Damn, that's good."

Rafe watched as she bit into her burger, groaned, and took another big bite. He'd never seen a woman eat like her. Not that he cared. He liked the way she enjoyed her food even if it was a fast-food burger and fries. She enjoyed everything to the fullest.

She grabbed the vanilla shake. "Why vanilla?"

Brianna took a long sip of her shake and then set it down. "Because chocolate is your favorite."

How did she know that? They hadn't been together that long. Who had she been talking to? Not that it mattered to him, but he was curious. They ate in companionable silence. When they were done, Rafe grabbed the empty plates and glasses and carried them into the kitchen before returning to Brianna.

"Bed time." He held out his hand.

Brianna put her hand in his, and he pulled her to her feet. She swayed for a moment and then was steady. Good. Her balance was back. Rafe led her to his bedroom.

"There are items in the bathroom for you, so go ahead and use the facilities."

"Thanks."

Rafe watched her go inside the bathroom and shut the door. He didn't know what to make of Brianna right now. She was shy but also spunky, yet she left him the chocolate shake, and when he asked her, she said because she knew it was his favorite.

With a shrug, he folded back the covers and waited.

* * * *

Brianna stared at herself in the mirror. "What are you doing?" she asked herself. Her hair was slightly mussed, but still in the braid she'd done earlier tonight. Her cheeks were flushed, and the blanket was still wrapped around her.

Damn. She'd gotten semi-naked in the club, but then remembered how Rafe made sure no one saw her. He'd been very careful when he restrained her to the cross, taking her bra off once she was in place.

The way the cross was set up, her breasts were between the two X's, and nobody could really see them. Even when they were done, although she was pretty out of it, she'd woken with blankets around her.

Rafe had been thoughtful about her concerns around her nudity, and it warmed her heart. After going to the bathroom, she brushed her teeth with the new toothbrush and toothpaste he'd left out for her.

There was a man's white t-shirt on the counter, as well. She shook it out. It would do. Undoing the blanket, she slipped the t-shirt over her head. It reached the top of her thighs. Why was she so shy around Rafe? It didn't make sense.

A yawn reminded her that was a conversation for another day. She folded the blanket and left it on the counter. Rafe was standing by the bed when she opened the door and walked out.

"All yours," she said, waving her hand at the open doorway.

He nodded. "Go ahead and climb in to stay warm." He walked past her and closed the door behind him.

Brianna shifted from one foot to the other. She was going to sleep in his bed? She fully expected to be in the guest room, not in his room—and not in his bed. She wasn't sure how she felt about this. It seemed like a very big step.

Was it that big of a deal? People slept with each other all the time. Brianna took a deep breath and let it out. It had been a while for her, mainly because, after her last relationship, she'd decided dating wasn't worth the bother.

She placed her hand on the mattress, feeling the soft sheets under her touch. *You can do this.* Brianna put her knee on the bed and climbed in. She slipped her feet beneath the top sheet and pulled it and the comforter over her body before resting her head on the pillow.

It smelled like Rafe. Probably his aftershave, but the scent was pleasant. She couldn't exactly pinpoint what the scent was. She shifted into a half-seated position as the bathroom door opened.

Rafe strode out in a pair of boxers. Her mouth watered as her gaze took in his sculpted chest, his trim waist, and… His cock was erect. She closed her eyes. What did she expect? Rafe hadn't had any pleasure this evening.

The mattress dipped. "Brianna," he said softly.

"Yes." She kept her eyes closed.

"Sweetheart, open your eyes and look at me please."

His request, made in such a tender way, caused her to opened her eyes, and she turned toward him. There was a smile playing around his lips, and there was mischief in his green eyes. "Thank you. Nothing is going to happen tonight."

"Huh?" What did he say? Her brain didn't comprehend the words.

"We're going to go to sleep."

"Sleep?" Why did she keep repeating what he's saying. "But…" Her gaze drifted to his groin.

"I'm fine." He pulled the covers over her lap. "You need to rest after your scene."

"I could have done that at home."

"You went into subspace for the first time with me. I want to be close in case you need me." He reached over and brushed his fingers against her cheek. "Have you gone into subspace before?"

"No." Was that why she'd felt so loopy earlier. "Was subspace that floaty feeling I had?"

"Probably. I've heard others describe it as floating; some say it's like an out of body experience; some feel nothing at all. Everyone is different."

"Oh." She pressed her cheek into his palm. "But you haven't been satisfied." While she didn't think she'd climaxed physically, her mind was completely satisfied, as was her body.

"This isn't about me." He shifted. "I received pleasure from watching you. I'm fine."

"Rafe," she started.

"This isn't up for discussion tonight." He removed his hand from her cheek, turned away, and turned off the light.

It took a minute for her eyes to adjust to the darkness. "I still don't think it's fair to you," she muttered.

"Come here." He slid his arm around her shoulder and pulled her to him. "Sleep in my arms, and I'll be more than happy."

Brianna snuggled against his warm skin. Her body fit perfectly against his, and her head rested in that area right below his shoulder but above his chest. "Night, Rafe."

"Night." He kissed the top of her head.

She laid there, going over the night's events, until sleep took her. For the first time in a long time, she felt safe and secure.

Chapter 10

Rafe woke refreshed and filled with joy. Brianna lay in his arms, sound asleep. She'd awakened once last night, confused. He gently reminded her of where she was and why. She shook her head and fell right back asleep.

He closed his eyes and took a deep breath. He could smell roses. Must be her shampoo. He hadn't had a relationship in years. Having Brianna here reminded him that he needed that connection. And now, because of her, he wanted it. Craved it, even.

She might fear fire, but she didn't fear him or what he did. Carefully he slid her out of his arms and onto the pillows, then slid out of bed, making sure to keep her covered.

He had a morning routine, and he liked sticking to it. He grabbed his running clothes, socks, and shoes and made his way into the bathroom. Once dressed, he found pen and paper, leaving Brianna a note before he went for his run.

The morning air was crisp. After warming up, he started out. It was Saturday, so he hoped, Brianna would spend the day with him. They could go to the club tonight and relax, no play. Then spend the night in his bed, and this time, maybe they'd make love.

Don't get ahead of yourself. He needed to give Brianna time. Their relationship was fairly new, and it wasn't like him to move this fast. Or was it? He'd had one-night stands before, but the other party knew the score. And he hadn't had one in a while. Rafe wasn't sure he knew what fast or slow meant in a real relationship.

Brianna meant more to him than a one-night stand. His heart was involved, and it had happened quicker than he expected. He let his thoughts wander as he ran. When he hit the park, he turned for home. By the time he arrived back at his house, he was hot and sweaty. He stepped into his house and groaned.

Fresh coffee teased his senses. "Brianna?"

"Hey." She popped her head around the corner of the kitchen. "Did you have a good run?" She sauntered up to him, looking bright and cheery this morning. She was wearing her street clothes from last night. Did she still have the thong on? His dick twitched.

"I did."

"I made coffee; I hope that's okay."

"It smells great. You can do whatever you want in my place."

"Good, because I took advantage of your absence and raided your fridge and pantry. What do you say to pancakes and bacon?"

"Perfect. Let me go get a shower." He leaned over and kissed her cheek before walking down the hallway. Inside his bathroom, he noticed a towel missing, and the inside of the shower was damp.

He grinned. Brianna had made herself at home. Good. That's what he wanted. He wanted her to be comfortable here and with him. He stripped and dropped his clothes in the hamper, then climbed in the shower and turned on the water.

Rafe made quick work of his shower and dressed. As he approached the kitchen, he could hear Brianna talking. "Okay, those are good. In the oven to keep warm, now for the bacon." She sighed. "You can do this; it's just a gas stove."

"Why don't you let me do that?" he asked. She was apparently uncomfortable with the appliance.

"I have it under control." She waved the package at him. "I poured you a cup of coffee." She tilted her head to the other counter where the mug sat.

He picked up the mug and took a sip. "Perfect. I'm sure you can handle the bacon, but let me." He took the bacon from her. "You did the hard part with the pancakes. I'm positive they're much better than mine." Rafe took another long drink of his coffee before setting it down.

Brianna laughed. "I wouldn't bet on that. I'll set the table then."

Rafe opened the bacon and turned the fire on under the pan. Brianna had used the electric griddle for the pancakes. While she could have done the bacon on the griddle, he preferred it on the stove. "Plates to the right of the fridge, silverware in the drawer below. Napkins in the holder on the breakfast bar." Brianna had moved away from the stove.

Rafe frowned. He had a gas stove. Was she that afraid of fire? He shook his head. She'd told him open flames bothered her. He turned his attention to the bacon.

"Got it."

There was a companionable silence as Rafe cooked the bacon, and Brianna set the table. "Do you want juice?" she asked.

"Not this morning, thank you. But feel free." He kept juice on hand for the mornings when he took his run and had to get to the firehouse. The juice helped him power through until he had breakfast with the guys.

"I'm good. I'm guessing butter is in the fridge, what about syrup?"

"Yes, butter in fridge. There's syrup in the pantry, second shelf toward the back." He glanced at Brianna as she walked into the pantry and came out with the bottle, shaking it at him, before grabbing the butter and putting the items on the table.

When she returned to the kitchen, she refilled both their coffee mugs and set them on the table, after adding milk and sugar to hers. Then she leaned against the doorframe to the pantry, close, but not too close, and watched him finish cooking the bacon. "You do that so effortlessly."

"What?" He placed a piece of bacon onto the paper towel to drain.

"Flip the bacon. I'm always afraid of getting splattered by grease."

"I've found the trick is to keep the fire on medium to low and use tongs instead of a fork." He finished removing the bacon from the pan and turned the burner off.

"Pancakes are in the oven. I put it on warm and covered them with foil so they wouldn't dry out."

"Great." He grabbed a platter, put the bacon on it, and then pulled the tray of pancakes out of the oven. Taking off the foil, he transferred them to the platter. He didn't mention the shape or color of them.

"I'm used to cooking on electric stove. The griddle was a little easier than the gas stove."

He glanced at her, and her cheeks were pink. "Even an electric griddle takes time to learn. Gas can be more efficient for some people." He carried the food to the table and placed it in the middle. "My lady." He held out a chair for her.

"Why thank you, kind sir." She sauntered over and sat.

Rafe barely contained himself when she said *kind sir*. They weren't in the bedroom or the club; the *sir* shouldn't cause his dick to pulse, but it did.

"Let's eat," he said, taking his seat.

* * * *

Brianna watched Rafe dig into the food. He didn't seem to mind that some of the pancakes were a little dark. If she was honest, they were almost burnt. When she woke and found herself alone, her first thought was that Rafe didn't like sleeping with her.

But then she saw his note, and her heart warmed. After cleaning up, she went into the kitchen. It took her a few minutes to figure out his complicated coffee maker, but once she did, she made a pot and then started looking around to see what she could make for breakfast.

At first, she felt like she was snooping, but in his note, he'd said, *make yourself at home*. Brianna had wanted to make breakfast for him. Rafe had calmed her when she woke in the middle of the night confused. He talked to her quietly, and she'd fallen back asleep, listening to his quiet voice.

Surprised at how energized she felt this morning, Brianna was ready to take on the world. Did that come from being with a man who put her needs first? Maybe. Rafe was tender, caring, and oh, so dominant.

A shaft of excitement shot through her veins. She

hadn't expected to feel so much from their scene. She'd have to talk to Ellie and ask her if this is how all women reacted.

"Brianna." Rafe's voice brought her out of her musings.

"Sorry."

"You were deep in thought. I asked if you would spend the day with me."

She bit her lip. Oh, how she wanted to say yes, but she had things she needed to do around her apartment, and she needed to complete her lesson plans for next week. "I want to, but unfortunately, I have work to do." The light in Rafe's eyes dimmed. Damn. "How about this." She leaned to the side so she could see the time on the microwave. "It's just ten. Take me home, and I'll come back at three. We can spend time together then. Will that work?"

"It will. Are you good with going to the club again tonight?"

"Sure."

"Good. Pack a bag."

"For what? I'll have clean clothes for the club."

"Because you're going to spend the night."

Her heart fluttered. Sure, she'd spent last night in his bed, but she had a feeling tonight wasn't going to be platonic. Was she ready for that? Her body screamed yes, but her brain told her to think about it. "Can I think about it?"

"Of course. I meant to ask earlier but was distracted by this wonderful breakfast. How are you feeling after last night?"

"Rested and ready to take on my day." She glanced at him. "And you can be honest about breakfast."

He sighed, stood, and crossed over to her. His hands were gentle when he pulled her from her chair and held her in front of him. "Look at me."

Brianna raised her chin; their gazes locked. She swallowed at the tempest in his gaze.

"It was wonderful because you made it for me."

"But I burnt the pancakes."

"I've done that a few times myself. I don't want you being upset over a few semi-burnt pancakes. You cooked for me, and I am appreciative."

She took a breath in surprise. "Thank you."

"Now let me get the dishes in the dishwasher while you gather your things." He brushed a kiss over her lips before releasing her.

Brianna watched him for a minute before she went into the bedroom to grab her bag. She'd put her club clothes in the bag earlier when she'd showered. Thank goodness she'd put a spare pair of underwear in.

When she walked back into the kitchen, Rafe had almost finished loading the dishwasher. "You're fast," she commented.

"That I am." He flashed her grin and shut the dishwasher before sauntering over to her. "Are you sure I can't convince you to stay?" he asked as he slid his arms around her waist.

She wanted to stay. That surprised her, but she shook her head. "I've got to get lesson plans done for next week, and if I don't do them today, they won't get done." She was aware if she spent the night with him tonight, she probably wouldn't get home until late tomorrow.

"All right." He kept an arm around her waist as he guided her to the garage after grabbing his keys off a hook next to the garage door.

The drive to her apartment was quiet. Once there, he parked in a visitor spot and walked her to her apartment. Funny how quickly she got used to him checking her place out before he'd allow her in.

"I'll pick you up at three," he said, pulling her close.

"I can drive to your place."

"I know, but please indulge me."

It was on the tip of her tongue to say okay, but what if she wanted to go home tonight instead of spending the night with him?

"I feel your hesitation. Am I moving too fast?"

"Yes, no…" She didn't know what she meant anymore. "What happens if I want to go home tonight?"

"Then I'll take you home."

"As simple as that?" Would he really do that? She'd heard horror stories about men abandoning a woman when she refused to go home with him.

"Yes." He cupped her cheek. "If you choose not to spend the night with me, I'll take you home. I promise you."

Brianna leaned against him. "I don't know what to think anymore." Her mind tried to sort out the pros and cons.

"Sweetheart." His voice was low. "I promise to be honest with you, and I always will be. You tell me you want to go home, I take you home. End of discussion."

She looked up at him. "So different."

"Better believe that." He brushed his lips over hers, but this time, she captured his mouth with hers. She wanted his kiss. A real kiss.

Rafe started in surprise but then took the kiss over. Her lips parted to allow his tongue to delve into her mouth. Oh yes, this was what she wanted. His kisses. His touch. The world melted away as they continued to kiss on her doorstep.

The slamming of a door made them jump apart. Brianna's face heated when she saw her neighbor walking down the hall.

"Good morning," Rafe said as the older woman passed them.

"Morning." The woman kept walking.

"That was embarrassing," Brianna commented.

"Why?" He kept her close.

"I…" She thought for a moment. "I have no idea."

"Good. But it's natural for us to kiss." He gave her another scorching kiss. "Go do what you need to do, and I'll be here at three." Her turned her in his arms and gave her a nudge into her apartment.

She glanced over her shoulder at him. "Bossy." Her voice was filled with laughter.

"Later." He pulled the door shut, and Brianna stood there, listening to his fading footsteps. It took her a few minutes to shake away the after effects of his kiss and head for her desk. She had things to do.

* * * *

Rafe parked in Sweet & Savory's parking lot. After leaving Brianna at her apartment, he called Max. He needed to talk to someone who enjoyed the lifestyle with a partner. Max had been in the longest relationship and was sitting at a table in the corner when he arrived.

"Can I get you something to eat or drink?" he asked, since he'd asked Max to meet him here.

"I've already ordered."

"Be right back." Rafe went up to the counter and ordered a cup of coffee. He was still full from breakfast, but coffee was always welcome. He returned to the table and sat down.

"What's up? You said you needed to talk to me about the lifestyle," Max said.

"Yes." Rafe cradled the coffee mug between his hands. "Here's the situation." He outlined to Max what had gone on between last night and this morning. "Am I moving too fast?"

One of the servers walked up to their table and set a plate in front of Max along with a bottle of water. "Anything else?" she asked.

"I'm fine," Max said.

"More coffee?"

"I'm good, thank you," Rafe said, and the server left.

Max took a bite of his sandwich and then looked at Rafe. "Rafe, we all move at our own pace. I can't tell you if you're going too fast or not. What did Brianna say?"

"She wanted to think about it." Rafe twirled his empty coffee mug.

"Not unusual. She's relatively new to the lifestyle in a practical sense."

"Yeah. But…" Rafe gathered his thoughts. "I don't know if this is normal in the lifestyle, but I have feelings for Brianna."

"I'm not surprised."

"What?" Rafe stared at Max.

"Rafe, I studied your questionnaire and hers before I gave them to you. You two fit well together. I knew you'd hit it off."

"Are you playing matchmaker?" Somehow, it didn't surprise him. All the women Max had paired up with Doms so far were in committed relationships.

"No. Most of the guys were already interested in their subs before they were put together at the club."

"I was interested even though Brianna and I had only met once before we met at the club."

"You did? Where?"

"Logan and I gave a talk at the elementary school where she teaches."

"I didn't know that." Max polished off his sandwich. "I'm going to tell you what I tell a lot of the Doms who come to me for advice. Be open and honest with Brianna. I watched your scene last night; you two have a connection that is rarer than you think."

"I'm being open and honest with her."

"And encourage her to be the same. My experience with Sierra was once she became comfortable with me and the lifestyle, things fell into place. Also, you say this whole relationship thing is new to you. Maybe it's new for her too."

Rafe nodded. He'd never considered or asked if Brianna had been in any long term, committed relationships. Though just the thought made him want to snarl.

"I talked with Zeke and Gabriel. They believe they'll have your fire play room ready in two weeks. Can you do a final walk through with them?"

"I can do it on Thursday after work or anytime on Friday when they're done." Anticipation flowed through Rafe. He was excited about this new venture with Max and the club.

"Okay. Do I need to provide you with any equipment?"

"Outside of what we've already discussed, no. I have all the supplies I need. I do have a question for you. What if there isn't enough interest in fire play? You went to a lot of expense to create the room." Rafe didn't like the idea that Max might have wasted his money.

"There's enough. Even if it's just to watch. I've had more than a two dozen members ask me about it. Even more since the room has been modified."

"You were always against it, so why now?" It had been part of the rules when he joined, which is why he only did it with his mentor or with specialized parties.

"Members were asking, and one of them is my wife. I reconsidered my stance, plus I spoke to King, and he made me aware how careful you are. That was enough for me."

"I'd forgotten you talked to King." Rafe shouldn't be surprised. A lot of people knew of the others in the lifestyle.

"Yeah, we go way back." Max grinned. "King mentioned to me he mentored you in fire play about two years ago so when the request came in, I decided it was time to chat with you."

Rafe shook his head. "Why am I not surprised?"

"I like keeping my finger on the pulse of my members and my club. Once we expanded, I knew members would start asking for other things. Especially when more people were interested in Anthony's knife play."

"He handles knives the way I do fire. With finesse and care."

"Which is why I asked you. Having the special room to do it in makes sense. I want us to be as safe as possible." Max sipped his water. "That also reminds me, are there any areas of the club that you see need attention?"

Rafe thought for a moment. "Not really. You have fire extinguishers around the club; there will be two in the fire play room. Lara is extra careful with the hot food and the small hot boxes to keep the food warm. You also keep tape over the cords so no one trips. Are you concerned about something you want me to look at?"

Max shook his head. "Not really, but let me know if you notice something. Since the expansion was never part of the original house, I wanted it to be seamless. My great-grandfather used the original as an illegal gambling den. When I inherited the property, I knew it would be great for a club; it just took some years to get it up and running."

"I'm glad you did. It gives us a safe space to play and has become quite popular."

"I know." Max rubbed his hand over the back of his neck. "People have asked me to open a second one."

"Are you?" That would be interesting.

Max shook his head. "I don't have the time or the resources. Not that I would stop anyone who wanted to open a club. There are more than enough people in the lifestyle to go around."

"But not everyone would run a club like you do." Max was very safety conscious. While there had been incidents, most were in the first months after Wicked Sanctuary had opened.

"Maybe and maybe not. This last thing with Ward has kind of made me wonder if I'm doing something wrong."

Rafe stiffened. "Ward was not your fault. I was there, Max. I've seen Ward in the club; nothing screamed predator. Some men are really good at hiding that side of themselves."

"As my wife keeps telling me."

"She's right. Max, you did all the right things when

you found out. By the way, what happened with him?" Rafe knew there had been an arraignment but hadn't had a chance to check in with Logan.

"His arraignment and hearing didn't go well. He went off at the judge, and the judge determined he was a danger to the community and kept him in jail. I believe his trial will be next year."

"And Emily seems to have bounced back." He'd seen her with Noah in the club.

"Emily is a lot stronger than any of us think. Hell, all the subs are. I think we Doms forget they have to be to put up with us."

Rafe laughed. But Max was right, subs were some of the strongest people he knew—and that included Brianna. He needed to remember that.

"Thanks, Max. I needed this."

"Anytime."

* * * *

Brianna stood in her bedroom, staring at her closet. Rafe asked her to pack a bag to stay at his house. Was she ready for this? Maybe that wasn't the right question. She'd already spent the night at his house.

Was she ready to make love with him? Her head screamed *yes*, but her heart was more hesitant. It wasn't like she hadn't been in a relationship before, but nothing like what she had with Rafe.

She'd heard the other subs talk about a connection between them and their Doms, and while Rafe was technically her first Dom, she'd felt the connection with him before she knew he was going to be her Dom.

That day at the school. Her entire being lit up when she made eye contact with him. Heck, she'd forgotten anyone else was around and where she was. But it still came back to whether or not she was ready to be intimate with Rafe.

A laugh escaped her lips. They'd already been intimate; they just hadn't had sex. He knew her body better than she did. Plus, he turned her on. His caring nature, the way he touched her body, and how he never expected more than she could give. Blowing out a breath, she grabbed a pair of sweats, jeans, and a shirt out of her closet.

After throwing them in the bag, she grabbed a night shirt, underwear, socks, and her cosmetic bag from the bathroom. That was enough. She glanced at the clock. Two-thirty. Not bad. She'd cleaned her apartment, made her lesson plans, and showered. Laundry could wait until after work next week.

Next, Brianna switched out the contents of her club bag. She grabbed a clean pair of boy shorts and a sports bra. That would work for tonight. Rafe hadn't mentioned what he wanted to do. She tapped her forefinger against her lips and threw a thong in there, as well.

She wasn't ready to go completely nude in the club yet but was surprised at how comfortable she felt being topless. Not that anyone had seen her topless, but it was less of a concern now that she'd done it. No one in the club judged others' bodies.

She'd always been a little self-conscious of her body. It would take time to get over her phobias, but Rafe was so good at working with her. She zipped up both bags and carried them to the front door.

Twenty-five minutes until three. Ugh. Going into the kitchen, she started making a grocery list. At least, she could get that out of the way. Next week after work was going to be busy, but that was okay. She'd rather spend time with Rafe.

By the time she'd finished her list and checked the fridge and what she had on hand, it was five minutes to three. The buzzer for entrance to the building went off. "Hello."

"Hi, beautiful, it's Rafe."

"Come on up." She buzzed him in, unlocked and opened her door, and waited for him. In a couple of minutes, he strode out of the elevator and down the hall to her.

"Ready?" he asked after brushing a kiss over her lips.

"Yes." Her lips tingled from his kiss. She leaned down to pick up her bags.

"I've got them." Rafe picked up the two bags.

Brianna grabbed her purse, then shut and locked the door. "So, what are we going to do this afternoon?" she asked. He hadn't said much, only that he wanted to spend the afternoon with her.

"Did you eat lunch?"

She shook her head. "I was still full from breakfast."

"How about a late lunch/early dinner? Then we can go to my place, relax, and change before we go to the club."

"Works for me."

"Where to?" He glanced over at her as he drove.

"I'd say Sweet & Savory, but Lara closes at three."

"She does, but she's catering the club tonight. Let me call and see if she'll let us stop by." Rafe stopped on the side of the road and pulled out his cell.

"Don't you have Bluetooth?"

"I do, but I prefer not to use it while driving unless it's an emergency."

Brianna nodded. "I don't want to put her out. Everyone needs time off." She didn't like the idea of putting Lara on the spot.

"We won't." He dialed her number. "Hey, Lara, Rafe. I know you're closed, but is there anyway Brianna and I can stop buy and grab some food?" The was a pause. "Great, thank you." Rafe hung up and looked at Brianna. "She's there along with Sierra, Crystal, and Regina and told us to come on down."

Within ten minutes, Rafe was pulling into the parking lot. Brianna reached to open the door when Rafe made a tsking sound. She pulled her hand back. Rafe stepped out of the SUV, jogged around and opened her door.

Brianna was still trying to get used to how Rafe always wanted to help her in and out of his vehicle. She turned toward the front door when Rafe stopped her. "Lara said to knock on the back door."

Brianna nodded. Rafe knocked, and a smiling Regina opened the door. "Hey, you two, come on in."

They made their way into Sweet & Savory, and Brianna almost burst out laughing. Sierra and Crystal were at the counters as if helping, but instead, their hands were in the air, and Lara was standing there, hands on hips with a frown. Regina stood behind Lara with a big grin on her face.

"Hey, Rafe, Brianna," Sierra said when she saw them.

Lara turned.

"You didn't need to stay open for us," Brianna said.

"It's fine." Lara waved her hand. "I'm just getting things ready for tonight, so I'm here anyway. Now, if I could just get these two to stop trying to help me." She glared at Sierra and Crystal.

"Sorry." They both backed away.

"You can get the stuff out of freezer. You'll see the boxes labeled for the club," Lara ordered.

Crystal and Regina scrambled off. Sierra grinned. "I'll take care of the paper products." She went into the other room.

"Now, what can I get for you two? And do you want it to go or eat here?" Lara asked.

"If it's not too much of an imposition, can we eat here? Brianna and I are going to chat about tonight over lunch, and it would be nice to do it without having to watch every word," Rafe said.

"No problem. Go grab a table wherever you want, but first, tell me what you want to eat."

"I want to keep it simple, what do you have that's easy?" Brianna said.

"The easiest right now would be the beef, bean, chicken wraps or bagel dogs."

"I'll take two bagel dogs," Brianna told her.

"Two chicken wraps for me," Rafe commented.

"You got it. Drinks?"

"Water, please," Brianna said.

"Same."

"Okay, go sit down, and I'll bring it over to you."

"You don't have to do that, Lara," Rafe said. "Just yell when ready, and I'll come get it. You're doing us a big enough favor." Rafe took Brianna by the arm and led her to a secluded table.

Brianna sat, and Rafe sat across from her. "I'm sure you're wondering what we're doing tonight?"

"A bit."

There was excitement in her eyes, and Rafe was glad

to see it. Some subs needed more time to recover from subspace, but Brianna seemed to have bounced back. "We're not going to scene tonight."

"We're not?" The surprise in her voice made him grin.

"No. You're still new to the lifestyle, and after going into subspace last night, I want to give your mind and body time to reset."

"I think I can understand that."

"We didn't talk a lot this morning. How are you feeling? Any aches or pains? Feeling out of sorts or anything like that?" He wanted to make sure she wasn't experiencing any negative aftereffects.

"Nothing hurts, and mentally, I feel great." She smiled. "I was energized when I got home; my apartment is sparkling clean, and my lessons plans for next week are done."

"That's great." He'd heard that some subs had lots of energy after subspace, and it looked like Brianna was one of them. Time would tell.

"Hey, Lara, do you have a fire extinguisher?" Sierra yelled.

Rafe jumped out of his seat as Lara pulled the extinguisher off the wall. "Where's the fire?" he asked.

"Dumpster outside the back door. I just went to throw the boxes in." Regina pointed at the door.

Rafe took the extinguisher from Lara. "Call 911." He bolted out the back door. Oh yes, they were going to need the fire department. Thank goodness, the dumpster was away from the building. After pulling the pin, Rafe directed the spray at the dumpster.

Within a few minutes, the fire truck pulled up. "Can't take a day off, can you, Lyons," the captain said.

Rafe backed away as they doused the fire. Had someone been careless and tossed a lit cigarette inside? It seemed odd to him that dumpster caught on fire. Within minutes, it was out; the guys poked around to make sure there were no lingering embers.

Lara, Crystal, Regina, and Brianna stood by the doorway. Brianna's eyes were wide, and the other women looked worried.

"All taken care of," Rafe said. "Lara, I can get the extinguisher refilled for you."

"Thanks, Rafe. I have extras just in case. I'm so glad I moved that dumpster away from the building."

He nodded. "You okay?" he asked Brianna.

"Fine. Just a little startled." She wrapped her arms around her waist.

"All is fine, ladies," the captain said. "Fire is out. Probably someone walking by dropped their cigarette in or a match."

"Thank you for responding so quickly," Lara said.

"We're here to serve." The captain nodded in Rafe's direction, climbed into the fire truck, and off they went.

"Well, that was exciting," Crystal commented.

"A little too much," Regina muttered.

"Agreed," Brianna said, her voice quiet.

"Let's all go back inside. I'll call the refuse company Monday and ask them to come pick it up." Lara stepped back inside the café.

"Before I leave, Lara, I'll push the dumpster to the other side of the parking lot." He didn't want it near her building.

"Thanks, Rafe."

Rafe took Brianna by the elbow and escorted her back to where they were sitting. "I'll go grab our food and water," he said after making sure she was seated.

"Lara, do you have cameras?" he asked. Something about that fire bothered him.

"Only at the back door, not around the building." He nodded. "Here's your food and drink. Take your time. I won't be leaving for at least another hour."

"Thanks." Rafe took the tray of food to the table. "Here we go." He took her plate and water and sat it in front of her, before putting his own food on the table.

"Smells so good," she said, picking up her bagel dog to take a bite.

"It really does." He picked up his chicken and chili wrap and dug in. The spicy chili hit his taste buds. They ate quietly for a few minutes.

"So, tonight?" Brianna asked.

"We'll basically hang out in the club. I'm not saying I won't touch you or anything."

"You said we wouldn't scene."

"Correct. We could watch some scenes or just sit a chat with our friends. We'll play it by ear, but I didn't want you to be disappointed when we don't scene."

"I'm not. I'm just worried…" Her words trailed off.

Rafe polished off his wraps. "Worried about what?"

"Don't you want to scene?" Her voice was so soft and tentative.

"There's more to the lifestyle than scening."

"I just thought…" Again, she broke off her words.

"Brianna, you can tell me anything. Communication is important."

She nodded. "I assumed you wanted to play tonight. I thought that's why I packed an overnight bag."

Rafe grinned. "I want to spend the night with you regardless if we play or not."

"Oh." Her cheeks flushed.

He reached across the table and placed his hand over hers. "Remember, no pressure, you call the shots. My place or your apartment. You have the right to tell me no."

She blinked at him. "I do, don't I?"

"Yes. You have the right to tell any man no, and they better listen."

"And if they don't?"

"They'll regret it."

* * * *

Brianna liked this protective side of Rafe. Even when he was putting out the dumpster fire, he made sure he put himself between the fire and the women. She knew he was protective, but it had really started to come out.

"Thank you." She turned her hand over in his and squeezed.

"For?"

"Being you." It was the truth. The men she'd been around hadn't been very open or honest with her, and that included her father.

"Now that we have that out of the way." He withdrew his hand and stood. "I'll clean up our lunch, and we can go back to my place. Or go for a drive. Your choice." He gathered their empty plates and water bottles.

Brianna watched him cross the room. He chatted with Lara for a minute before returning to the table. She was so enthralled watching him move with such grace she didn't realize for a moment he was standing next to her, holding his hand out.

"Always a gentleman," she said, placing her hand in his.

"I was raised right." He helped her to her feet. They

bid Lara good bye and walked out the back door. "Give me a minute to move the dumpster?"

"Do you want help?" she asked.

"I'm good." He touched the dumpster, then maneuvered behind it, and pushed it across the small lot. He dusted his hands off before walking back to her. "That's done."

"Why did you feel the need to move it away from the café?"

"To be safe." He opened the door to his SUV for her. "I know the fire is out, but I'd rather Lara doesn't worry about it."

Brianna nodded. He was so considerate.

"Are we going back to my place or for a drive?" he asked after they were in his vehicle.

"How about we drive out and sit by the water?" She loved Puget Sound and wasn't quite ready to go back to his place.

"Anything you want." He pulled out of the parking lot and headed west. In about twenty minutes, he parked close to the beach. "Do you want to walk?"

She glanced out the windshield. It wasn't raining. It was cool, but she didn't mind the cold. "I'd like that."

"Okay. Good. I think I threw two jackets in the car." He climbed out and opened the back door.

Brianna got out of the vehicle as Rafe walked around, holding out a red puffy jacket to her. "Put this on so you don't freeze."

He held out the jacket, and she slipped her arms into the sleeves as he pulled it over her shoulders then moved in front of her and zipped it up.

"This has to be yours." There was laughter in her voice as she pushed the sleeves up so she could find her hands.

"Guilty." He captured her hand, and they began to walk the trail. "I haven't been down here in a while."

"I've only been here once."

The walked in silence for a few. "Rafe, where do you see this…" She waved her hands. "…with us going?" She'd been thinking about this.

"That's really up to you."

"What do you mean?" She wasn't sure what he meant by that. Well, in a way she did.

"I mean, we can continue as we are right now, playing in the club and being friends out of the club." He paused and glanced over at her. "Or we can play in the club and have a relationship outside of it."

"Relationship?" Is that where this was heading? Who was she kidding? They were already in a relationship. She'd slept in his arms, and while some may not consider that a relationship, she did.

"Yes." He tugged her to a stop. "In case you have any doubt, I want to have a relationship with you in and out of the club."

"We barely know each other." Why was she arguing with him?

"I believe I know you better than you think." He ran his fingers over her cheek. "You love your job; your apartment is cozy. You enjoy being with the women in the club, and you and I fit together."

"We do." She grinned. He nailed it. They fit.

"Good. So…" His cell started ringing. He pulled it out of his pocket. "Sorry, I need to take this?"

"Sure."

"Hey, Captain, what's up?"

Brianna started to pull away, but Rafe tightened his

hand on hers and shook his head.

"Yeah, sure. What time? All right, see you there on Monday." He slipped his phone back in his pocket.

"Work issue?"

"Just a meeting that got scheduled."

"Do they often do that to you?" She really didn't know that much about his job.

"No." They continued walking. "We've had a string of suspicious fires over the past few months. My boss was just giving me a heads up about a meeting."

"Like the one at Lara's?"

"I think the one at Lara's was probably an accident. Some of the others we've had seem to be deliberate."

"Will you tell me about them?"

"You don't really want to hear about my job. You dislike fire."

"And you love it. I'd like to know more about what you do."

Rafe nodded. "All right. It started with a fire a couple of months ago."

Brianna listened to Rafe as they walked. She learned about his suspicions over some of the fires and asked him questions about how he could tell if a fire was arson or not. She heard the passion in his voice as he spoke.

It was more than that. He liked figuring out puzzles. And while she wasn't comfortable with open flame, Rafe had an understanding of fire that Brianna admired.

"Will you tell me more about the fire play you're planning on doing at the club?" She was curious about it.

"While it's considered fire play, I will mainly be doing fire cupping."

"What is that?"

"It's basically taking fire and trapping it in a cup and

adhering the cup to someone's skin."

She shivered. "Sounds painful."

"It's not. If you watched the Olympics, you might have seen athletes with circular red marks on their backs or arms."

"Oh yeah, I remember that."

"That is fire cupping. It's great for relieving pain, increasing circulation, and removing toxins from the body. Many like it to relax and let themselves go in a safe situation."

"Have you done a lot of it?" This was interesting. Not that she wanted to try, but it was intriguing.

"I've been studying fire since I was a teenager. I've been doing fire play and fire cupping for the last eight years. I'm no master, but I'm very competent at it."

"You're competent at a lot of things." They'd reached the end for the trail, so they turned and started back.

"I'm glad you think so." He squeezed her hand. "The fire play room will be ready in probably another week or so. I'll check it out again before I bring any of my equipment from home."

"You have equipment?"

"I have fire cupping sets along with everything I need to make it a pleasurable experience."

"Why such a specialized room if it's safe?"

"Because you can never be too safe, and I don't want anything to happen to the club. Plus, by now, you should understand that I'm very much into fire safety."

"Yes. You are." She loved how much he was into safety. That was part of the reason his being a firefighter didn't bother her. "I like that."

"I'm glad you got the counseling to deal with the

aftermath of the fire you were in. Is there anything else about that day that bothers you?"

"How did you know?" There were still some fears lingering in the back of her mind.

"I've watched how you react, and well, I sensed you were holding something back."

Brianna shivered. "I told you about my cousin, but I left something out."

"Will you tell me?"

"He liked playing with matches." Now she knew he was a pyromaniac, but she didn't at the time.

"How old was he?"

"Fifteen."

"Old enough to know better."

"Yeah." She took a deep breath. "He was more than a pyro. He… I think he wanted to hurt someone. Me." Her voice grew small. "I said I ran for the closet. I didn't. He pushed me in there." She swallowed; now, he knew the secret that only her therapist knew. "You know the rest."

Rafe swore under his breath. "Ass."

She nodded.

"He left you in the closet, started the fire, and ran?" It wasn't really a question.

She nodded, unable to raise her head.

"You should have told someone."

"I—I couldn't." Brianna raised her head, straightening. "Anyhow, it's a moot point because he can't hurt anyone now."

"He's dead?"

She nodded "He died in prison."

Rafe stopped walking and pulled her into his arms. "You've been through a lot. It's okay to be scared of fire.”

“It’s really open flames that get to me. Gas stoves bother me a bit. Which is why I used the electric griddle at your place.”

“I get that.” They’d made it back to his SUV. Rafe pulled her into his arms. “If I ever make you uncomfortable with fire, tell me.”

“I will.”

Brianna felt better talking more about what had happened. She allowed Rafe to help her back into his vehicle.

“I don’t remember—what happened to your cousin after the fire and the fireman got you out?” he asked.

“Nothing that I was aware of. I do know my parents never invited my aunt and uncle back, even when we got a new place to live.”

“Good. You didn’t need to live with that fear.”

“My parents didn’t understand my fear.”

“What?” He turned to her in his seat.

“They couldn’t understand why I couldn’t let go of my fear of an open flame.”

“God, Brianna, I’m so sorry.”

She shrugged her shoulders. “They weren’t very understanding, and I dealt with it the best I could.”

“No child should have to deal with it. Please tell me they got you counseling?”

“They did for a little bit. My parents kept saying I’d get over it.” She looked out the windshield. “But I never really did. I had nightmares for years.”

“Of course, you did.”

“I realized when I went to college I needed more help and got counseling there and later with a private therapist.”

"I'm glad." He turned back in his seat and started the engine. "I'm here if you have nightmares or just need to talk. No judgment."

Brianna glanced over at Rafe. Maybe it was time to tell him the rest of it. Tell him about her college boyfriends. She stared out the window as they pulled away from the water. Not today. Today, the rest of it, was for enjoying time with him. He was so different from those guys. So much better than they were. Rafe treated her like she mattered.

Chapter 11

Rafe drew Brianna into his arms as they watched a scene with Rose and Oliver. He couldn't get out of his mind what Brianna had told him. Rafe was angry at her parents for belittling her fear. Not everyone could handle fire.

Brianna might be afraid of fire, but she wasn't afraid of him or what he did. That, all by itself, opened his heart to strong feelings for her. She trusted him. He would not take that lightly.

With fire cupping, there really wasn't an open flame, but if someone wanted him to use a fire wand, then there would be. He'd cross that path when they came to it. Plus, he wouldn't do that with just anyone.

That was another thing he needed to talk with Brianna about. He would be touching other people to prepare their skin, or in the case of fire wands, to remove the fire. He'd remind her there was nothing sexual about it for him, unless he was playing with her. She aroused him. Not the fire play. Her.

Brianna shifted, and Rafe glanced down at her. Her eyes were closed. He glanced at the stage. Oliver was caressing Rose's breasts, nothing she hadn't seen before in the club.

"Brianna, what's wrong?" he asked.

She opened her eyes. "Nothing, Sir."

"You had your eyes closed."

"Yes." She shifted again. "Please look where your hands are, Sir."

Rafe glanced down. He was cupping her breasts, his fingers squeezing and playing with her nipples. He hadn't even realized he was doing it. "Am I hurting you?"

"No, Sir. I'm aroused."

He could see that by her squirming. "As you should be." He flicked his index finger against her nipples.

"Rafe… Sir."

The pleasure in her voice made him grin. "Do you want to go to my place?" They'd been at the club for a couple of hours now, and he was ready to take her home and to his bed.

"Yes, please, Sir."

Rafe kept his arms around her and walked backward, away from the scene, before releasing her. "Let's go." They said a brief goodnight to Zeke and Allyson. After quickly changing, they were in Rafe's SUV, headed for his home.

Brianna kept wiggling. "What's going on, wiggle worm?" It wasn't like her to be like this.

"I…"

He halted at a stop sign and looked at her. Brianna stared at him, and the next thing he knew, she undid her seat belt, and her lips were on his. Rafe didn't hesitate; he wrapped his hand around her neck and deepened the kiss.

A knock on the driver's window broke the kiss. He whipped his head around to see a grinning Colby on his motorcycle with Lara behind him.

"Get a room," Colby yelled, before he checked the road and took off.

Rafe laughed, and Brianna groaned. Her cheeks were

pink. Not saying a word, he took her hand and put it on his thigh as he drove his place. They made it in record time.

He'd barely turned the engine off when Brianna slid across the seat to exit on the passenger side. Rafe jumped out and rounded the back of his SUV just as Brianna's feet hit the ground, and she shut the door.

"Now, you're mine," he said. Bending down, he caught her around the waist and lifted her onto his shoulder, caveman style.

"Rafe." There was laughter in her voice.

"You're mine tonight." He marched with her over his shoulder into the house and straight to his bedroom. Once there, he set her on her feet.

"You're being a little cavemanish."

"Yes, I am." He brushed a kiss over her lips. "Stand here while I undress you."

"Yes, Sir."

His dick jumped. It was the first time she used Sir in a sexual situation outside the club. Oh, they were going to have fun tonight.

* * * *

Brianna's nerves tingled at Rafe's words. Surprised when he threw her over his shoulder and carried her inside, all she could do was laugh. He'd been teasing her from the moment they'd walked into the club, and she'd had enough.

She wanted him more than she'd ever wanted anyone. When he ordered her to stand while he undressed her, the words "Yes, Sir" slid from her lips naturally. His eyes flared with heat and desire.

"Why did you bother to put your street clothes on?" he asked as he peeled her t-shirt up and over her head.

153

"Because I'm not about to go running around in a bra and boy shorts." She pushed a strand of hair away from her face.

"I like how you dress in the club, but I bet you're fantastic with nothing on at all." He unfastened her jeans and began sliding them down her legs. "Shoes," he muttered, before lifting one foot and palming the shoe off then doing the same with the other foot.

"Step out," he said when her jeans pooled around her ankles.

Brianna did as he said. Heat filled her. She wanted to touch Rafe, but he had too many clothes on. When he straightened, she reached for the hem of his t-shirt.

His hands covered her. "Impatient, are we?"

"Yes, I am, Sir."

"Too bad." He removed her hands. "This will go my way."

She stuck her lower lip out in a pout but let her hands fall back to her sides.

"Good girl. Now, let's get rid of this bra." He undid the front fastening and pulled the straps from her arms. Her bra was flung in the direction where he'd thrown her t-shirt earlier.

He cupped her breasts and tapped his index finger against her stiff nipple. A moan left her lips, and her head fell back at the sensations running through her body.

"I like that sound," he said softly as his fingers trailed over her stomach to the top of her boy shorts. He slid them down her legs. "No thong tonight?"

"No." She'd decided at the last minute to go commando under the boy shorts. Which maybe hadn't been such a good idea since the seam had teased her clit every time she moved.

"If I had known that…" His hands skimmed up her legs and back to her waist. "When did you plan on telling me?"

Brianna bit her lower lip. "I wasn't."

"Minx." He gave her a brief hard kiss before grasping her by the waist and tossing her onto his bed.

Brianna couldn't help but laugh, but her laughter died when she saw the smoldering look in Rafe's eyes. Desire and need flared in his beautiful gaze. She rolled onto her side and watched him as he undressed.

He swept his t-shirt up and over his head, showing off his six-pack abs and strong shoulders, before kicking off his shoes. The he pushed his pants off. The same ones he wore in the club.

"You were commando too?" Brianna noted as his cock bounced after being released from the fabric.

"Around you I am." His long legs carried him over to the bed.

Rafe knelt on the mattress. "Now, I have you at my mercy." He pounced.

Brianna laughed as he pushed her onto her back and placed kisses all over her face. "Oh dear, please be gentle."

His grin widened. "You are mine, and I will do what I want."

"Oh yes, Sir."

The gleam in his eyes brightened. "Arms over your head and legs spread."

She didn't even hesitate. Anticipation and desire flowed through her body. She wanted Rafe.

"Can you keep your arms above your head, or do I need to restrain them?" His voice was deep and husky.

"I can keep them there." At least she hoped so.

"Good." He straddled her upper thighs, his hard cock resting on her mound. Rafe leaned over and began running kisses over her face, her neck, and to the valley between her breasts, before his lips closed over one nipple while his fingers played with the other one, then he switched.

Her fingers curled into her palms as fire swept from her nipples to her clit. "Rafe."

"Arousal suits you." He kissed his way over her belly as he scooted down between her legs. When he reached the top of her mound, he gave it a little kiss before licking her slit.

"Damn," she muttered, squirming on the bed.

"You like that?" Before she could answer, he did it again, but this time, he pushed her folds apart with his tongue.

Her breath caught in her throat as sharp flashes of pleasure shot through her. His hands were on her inner thighs and pushed outward. "Pretty pussy," he murmured before lowering his head.

Brianna lost what little breath she had in her lungs as her pussy muscles tightened at his lick. He paused and used his tongue to toy with her clit. She shook her head, trying to find the words for how she felt, but nothing came to her.

* * * *

Rafe glanced up at Brianna and grinned. Her eyes were closed, her breathing shallow, and her fingers curled into the quilt. She probably didn't even realize she'd lowered her arms. He wondered how far he could push her before she begged.

He held her open and his tongue dove in, licking, and thrusting into her. Her hips wiggled. Can't have that. He placed his hands on her hips, stilling her as he continued his assault.

"Rafe...I..." Small tremors shook her body. Rafe didn't let up, knowing her climax was close. It would only be the first of several tonight. Brianna let out a small cry as she orgasmed. He could only smile on the inside at her soft moans.

Raising his head, he kissed the top of her mound and slid up her body until his dick was at her entrance. He rubbed the head of his cock through her wetness.

"Please, Rafe."

"Begging already?"

"Yes. I need you."

"Then you shall have me." He shifted and reached for a condom.

"You don't need it."

Rafe gazed down at her. "Are you sure?"

"Yes."

He shifted his hips and slipped into her wetness.

Brianna whimpered as he filled her. Her eyes fluttered shut as he began to move. He kept his gaze on her face as her pussy tightened around his cock. She felt so good gripping him. This was meant to be.

He didn't pause to think about anything other than that, right now, all he cared about was Brianna's pleasure. This woman deserved it and more.

"Rafe, more, please." Her soft voice was music to his ears. He shifted his hips and moved faster. "So tight."

"Just for you."

Those words wrapped around his heart. If he wasn't already infatuated with her, this would have sealed the deal. Heck, who was he kidding? He was half-way in love with her. It seemed quick, but it wasn't. Brianna was special.

"I'm going to come."

"You may come, but that doesn't mean I'm going to stop." Her pussy tightened around his dick. Damn, it was almost as if she was trying to milk him, to make him come.

Rafe brushed the hair away from her face as he held still, letting the tremors coursing through her to settle.

"You feel so hard." Her hot breath brushed over his skin.

"I'm always hard for you." He adjusted his hip.

"How? Men don't stay this hard."

He laughed. "Maybe the men in your past, but I have great control."

"Fuck," she whispered.

"That's what I plan on doing." He pulled back and plunged into her, again and again. After her third climax, Rafe knew it was time.

"Stop. I can't." Her head thrashed against the mattress.

"Are you safewording out?" He wanted to make sure he understood.

"No. I…" She screamed as another climax hit her. This time, Rafe kept fucking her, allowing his orgasm to rise.

"Yes," he cried out as his balls tightened and he let go.

His cock pulsed with his orgasm. Rafe gathered her into his arms as she tightened around him. He held her close as their climaxes flowed through them.

"Brianna?" She went lax in his arms. "Baby, are you okay?"

"You've killed me." Her voice was soft.

"We've barely scratched the surface."

"Sleep, I need sleep."

"Anything you want, love."

* * * *

Rafe woke with Brianna curled up in his arms. Damn. This woman had kept up with him last night, and it was more than pleasure that flowed through him. With care, he maneuvered her head to the pillow, and her body onto the mattress.

He climbed out of bed, and walked into the bathroom. Energy flowed through his body. That's what sex with the right woman could do for a man.

A grin spread across his lips. Brianna was definitely the right woman for him. She matched him both in and out of bed, as well as in Wicked Sanctuary. It didn't bother him she didn't want to do fire play; it wasn't for everyone. He enjoyed doing demos and teaching about it, so he'd be fine.

Stepping outside the bathroom with a towel around his waist, he glanced at the bed to see Brianna watching him.

"Good morning," he said.

"Morning." She shifted and her hair fell over one shoulder.

"I'm going to dress and get us breakfast." Her cheeks turned pink and Rafe grinned. "There's nothing to be embarrassed about." He crossed to the bed, sat, then ran his finger over her blushing cheek.

Brianna bit her lip. "Morning afters are embarrassing." She shifted the sheet higher.

"Not anymore. We are consenting adults, and we enjoy sex." He stared at her. "You did receive pleasure last night, didn't you?"

"Of course I did." Her quick answer settled the tiny doubt that had been flowing through him.

"Good." He brushed a kiss over her lips. "Breakfast in twenty. I suggest you get up and get dressed." He stood.

"But you're not dressed." Her eyes danced with mischief as she stroked the place where he was just sitting.

"Don't tempt me." Rafe knelt on the bed and gave her ass a swat. "Get dressed. I have a fun day planned for us."

"Oh?" She squirmed.

"Yes. Now behave." He gave her another swat before moving away and pulling a pair of sweats out of the dresser. "Twenty minutes, and don't be late."

"Yes, Sir."

Chapter 12

The last two weeks had passed quickly, Brianna thought as she closed her classroom door on a Thursday afternoon. Between teaching and spending time with Rafe, she barely had any time to herself, and she didn't mind at all. She was falling for Rafe. There was no stopping it. Over these past weeks, he'd shown her pleasure she had never known, both inside and outside the club.

She explored her wants and needs with him and enjoyed herself. Even though tonight was Thursday, they were going to the club. Not to play but so Rafe could demonstrate fire cupping. They'd had a long talk about it this past weekend.

He'd wanted her to understand while he would be touching other people, it wasn't for sensuality's sake. It was so the fire cupping was enjoyable for them. She was fine with that. Right now, she wasn't comfortable enough to try it, but she wouldn't begrudge other people wanting to.

Once inside her car, she drove home. She really only spent time at her apartment during the week when Rafe was at work. They usually spent Friday nights, Saturdays, and Sundays together. During the week, it was easier for Rafe to be home alone, what with his work hours, but that didn't mean they didn't have dinner together.

Not that Brianna minded. It wasn't like they didn't talk or text each other during the days they weren't together. Some might think the schedule wasn't a good one for a relationship, but for them, it worked.

Once home, she grabbed her mail, took a quick shower, and changed. In a way, she was excited to see the fire cupping demo. Last Sunday, Rafe had taken her on a walk-through of the room Max had built at the club, and shown her his equipment. Nothing looked that dangerous.

He'd also shown her all the precautions he'd put in place to make sure everyone would be safe, not only those watching, but those experiencing fire play. Brianna was proud of herself for listening to Rafe and not panicking.

Maybe because Rafe took the time to understand her fears and not belittle her for them as her family had. She'd just finished putting her purse and cell inside her bag for the club when the buzzer to the apartment building rang.

She glanced at the clock. Rafe was early, but he had taken the afternoon off so he could be prepared for tonight, and they were going to dinner before the club.

"Hello."

"Hey, sweetheart." Rafe's voice was husky.

"Come on up." She pressed the buzzer and then opened her apartment door. Maybe it was time to talk about getting him keys to her place. This way he wouldn't have to buzz her every time he wanted to visit.

The elevator door opened, and Rafe sauntered down the hall with a big grin on his face. Once he reached her, he drew her into his arms, and they kissed. She enjoyed being greeted this way. Funny how quickly she'd become accustomed to Rafe's kisses and his touch.

"Are you ready for tonight?" he asked after breaking the kiss.

"Yes." She grabbed her bag, and they were off.

The club was buzzing when they arrived at seven-thirty. They parted ways to change, and Rafe told her to meet him in the club when ready.

"You're here," Sierra exclaimed when she saw Brianna.

"Yes, I wouldn't miss this." Brianna stripped off her street clothes and put them in her bag and then put the bag into a locker. She looked at Sierra. "I have a favor to ask." She'd been thinking about this for a while.

"Sure. Shoot."

"Would you help me shop for new club clothes?" Brianna had noticed how Sierra, Crystal, and a lot of the other subs dressed or didn't dress. She wanted to spice things up for Rafe.

"I'd love to. Does this mean you and Rafe are official?"

Brianna laughed. "I guess so. We've been together…" She counted the weeks in her head. "It's only been seven weeks."

"It doesn't take long with these men." Sierra smiled. "When are you available?"

"Not until after four on weekdays."

"I can work with that. Since we have each other's phone numbers, why don't I call you next week and set something up."

"That works." Brianna had been thinking about her clothing. She was getting comfortable in the club and, several times, had allowed Rafe to remove her bra while they scened. While she wasn't ready to be nude in the club, she was thinking about wearing a little more revealing clothing. Rafe would love it.

Brianna and Sierra walked into the club and over to the room where the fire play would happen. Rafe was already pulling things out of the cabinet, and there was a good crowd.

"Ladies," Max said, coming up to them. "Brianna, Rafe asked me to look after you tonight."

"Oh." She glanced at Rafe, who winked at her. "And who is going to look after Sierra, Sir?"

"I'm Rafe's demo sub tonight."

No wonder Sierra was practically bouncing out of her skin.

"Rafe assured me that you were okay with it." Max frowned.

"It's fine, Sir. He didn't mention to me that Sierra was his demo partner tonight, but we talked about it."

"All right, Sierra, my love." Max drew her into his arms. "Enjoy yourself and listen to Rafe."

"I will, my love, my Sir." Sierra went up on her toes and kissed Max before moving into the scene space with Rafe.

Max led Brianna to an area close to the front. "Rafe told me he'll explain everything he's doing."

Brianna's heart warmed. Rafe had gone over this demo with her several times. Now, he had Max with her to make sure she would be okay. Rafe thought of everything.

At eight, Rafe raised his hands, and the room quieted down. "Evening, everyone. Tonight, I'm going to demo fire cupping. Let me start off by saying that you need to learn and understand how this works before trying to do it yourself. I've studied with a fire play master for the last eight years."

"Will you be giving classes?" someone called out.

"I haven't thought about it." Rafe waved his hand. "For now, it will just be demos. Sierra has graciously volunteered to be my demo sub for tonight."

"That's a good word for it," Crystal yelled.

"Bite me, bitch," Sierra grinned at her friend.

Brianna loved the camaraderie of the group. They might call each other names, but it was all in good fun.

"While Sierra gets ready, let me explain that fire cupping is used in a lot of sports medicine and has medicinal uses. Tonight, that's what this is about."

Sierra walked up to Rafe, topless and in boy shorts. He helped her onto the table.

"This is something you want to do outside on concrete. If you're inside, do this on tile." He tapped his foot. "Max graciously built this room. Everything is fire resistant or fireproof."

Brianna kept her gaze on Rafe and what he was doing. "On my side table here, I have everything I need for fire cupping. I keep all my fire supplies on one side and the fire dousing supplies on the other."

She shifted from one foot to the other. Fire dousing supplies sounded serious.

"Basically, I have a bottle of water, cotton towels to smother the fire, a bucket of water, and of course, a fire extinguisher, if needed. Fire supplies include my wands, the fire cups, oil, and alcohol."

That didn't sound too bad.

"What kind of alcohol are you using?" someone asked.

"I use isopropyl alcohol at seventy percent. That is the best and least likely to burn the skin." He picked up the bottle of oil. "Now, I'm going to generously spread this over Sierra's back." Rafe poured it onto Sierra's back and began rubbing it in. "This will allow the cups to get suction but also allow me to move the cups as needed."

Sierra let out a little moan as he massaged the oil into her skin.

"Tops, this can be very sensual for your bottom. Giving them a massage will help them relax." Rafe lifted his hands and dried them on a towel. "Since this is Sierra's first time, I'm going to start with smaller cups, and as she gets used to the sensations, after a few sessions, we can move up to bigger ones."

Brianna watched as Rafe picked up one of the wands. "Basically, the wand is made of cotton balls and cheese cloth. I've sprayed it down well with alcohol." He picked up a lighter and flicked it on.

Brianna jumped as the cotton caught fire. "Now, I'll run the wand inside the cup and place it on her body." Brianna's gaze was steady on Rafe as he ran the wand fairly quickly around the rim of the cup, and he placed it on Sierra's back. He did two more before dousing the fire in the water bucket. Brianna's eyes stayed on the bucket until she was sure the fire was out.

"As you can see, the skin is rising in the cup. How are you doing, Sierra?"

"Fine, it feels so different."

"Many use fire cupping for sore muscles, which is good. In this case, we're doing it more to promote better circulation and sensations." Rafe slid one cup down Sierra's back, then moved another one.

"While there is heat trapped inside the cup, it is warm, but not hot. The last thing you want to do is burn the skin, and it can happen. Not so much with fire cupping but with other types of fire play."

Rafe moved the cups around before taking them off. There were red circles on Sierra's back. "Because this is new to Sierra, the cups are left on for three minutes. After several sessions, I can increase the time. These circles will disappear within ten days and should not be painful." Rafe took a towel and wiped it over Sierra's back, removing any residual oil from her skin. "And that is fire cupping."

Everyone clapped, and Rafe helped Sierra off the table. She was grinning ear to ear as she walked over to Max, her breasts bouncing. Max glanced over at Brianna as he pulled Sierra into his arms.

"I'm fine, Sir," Brianna said.

Max nodded and guided Sierra over to the aftercare area. Brianna watched Rafe as he cleaned up the area while answering questions from club members. She'd been a bit nervous when he lit the fire, but she watched how he handled everything and how careful he was.

She shook her head. Of course, he was careful. Rafe knew as well as she did how destructive fire could be. Brianna glanced up and found Rafe staring at her. She smiled at him, and he winked at her, which warmed her more than anything.

It was almost another full hour before everyone's questions were answered, and Rafe joined her. "What did you think?" he asked.

"Very interesting, Sir. Sierra looked dreamy when she finished."

"It can have that effect on some people. Most feel very relaxed."

"I enjoyed watching it, Sir."

"I'm glad. Let's say good bye to everyone, so I can get you home. You have to teach tomorrow."

Brianna nodded. Rafe was so considerate of her time and making sure she got enough rest. It was nice to let go, to have someone look after her for a change.

She could definitely get used to this.

Chapter 13

"All right class," Brianna said on Friday afternoon. "Let's have silent reading time." They only had about forty-five minutes left in the day.

All the sudden, there was a huge bang. Brianna jumped up from her desk and looked outside the window of her class door. Smoke. Was there a fire? The thought barely flitted through her mind when the alarm went off.

She froze, and her mind went back to being in that closet. Cries of her kids pulled her out of the memory. Blowing out a breath, she tried to calm her racing heart. This wasn't the time to panic. Pushing her fear aside, she grabbed her phone from her desk. "Okay, kids. Line up."

"What was that noise, Miss Brianna?" one of the girls asked with a tremor in her voice.

"I don't know. Everything will be fine." The kids lined up. Brianna opened her classroom door. While there was smoke, she didn't see any flames. She glanced at the exit strategy beside the door to refresh her memory, though she didn't need it. She never entered a building or room without knowing the exits. Never again.

"All right, kids, we're going to leave the classroom now. We'll go right and out the back door to our assigned area on the playground. Stay in formation and remember to hold hands." She looked at Matt. "Matt, you're in the lead."

"Yes, Miss Brianna. This way everyone." Holding hands, her kids walked out of the classroom, and she brought up the rear. The other classes were leaving, as well. They were a small school, so there weren't many classrooms in this school, only six.

At the back door, the assistant principal held it open and directed the children away from the building. Brianna's heart pounded as she made her way behind her class and out of the building. Everything inside her said "run". She held up her hands, not surprised that they were shaking badly. This was her worst nightmare. As she followed her class through the door, she breathed a huge sigh of relief to be outside. The farther away from the school they got, the more that relief took hold. They were okay. She was okay.

Once they were away from the building and in the open grass area, she noticed that several of the girls were crying. "Everything will be okay." She sat down on the grass and opened her arms.

Her students swarmed her, and that was fine. She knew their fear, and while they'd had drills, this was different. What they needed now was a distraction. She could use one too. "Let's sing." Brianna started singing the ABC song. One by one, the kids started singing with her.

Soon, the entire school was singing as fire trucks arrived. It was Friday, but Brianna noticed Rafe step out of the first truck. Several firefighters immediately went inside. Brianna kept her gaze on Rafe as he stood by the truck, chatting with another man.

She relaxed more. They did not seem overly concerned, so maybe this was nothing. But it wasn't a drill either. After about five minutes, the firefighters walked out of the school and straight over to Rafe and the other man.

The principal and assistant principal joined them. After a few minutes of discussion, both women shook their heads and walked back toward the students. The principal clapped her hands, and the singing stopped.

"False alarm, everyone. Not sure who, but someone threw a smoke bomb in the hall."

Brianna took a deep breath, letting the last vestiges of her panic go.

"The school buses will be here shortly to take you all home. If you need to grab anything from your classroom, a firefighter will escort you. We've got the doors open to air out the smoke."

Just then, the school buses rolled up. Brianna stood and gathered her students. "Is there anything you need that can't stay in the classroom until Monday?"

Two hands shot up.

"My bag has my medicine in it," Jessie said.

"I didn't eat my lunch today, and it will spoil," Matt said.

"Okay. I'll run in and get them." Brianna looked up to see Rafe walking toward her. "I want you all to go stand with Miss Ruby's class until I come back." She watched her kids until Ruby looked up.

Ruby gestured as if she was slinging something over her shoulder and Brianna realized she was signaling she needed her purse, and Brianna waved. That would be easy enough to get as their classrooms were right next to each other.

"You need to go inside?" Rafe asked.

"Yes." She was happy to see him.

"I'll escort you." His tone was so serious.

"Thank you."

Rafe took her by the arm, and they walked in the door she'd come out of. The smoke was already clearing. She stopped at Ruby's classroom.

"I thought yours was the next one," Rafe commented.

"It is. I'm grabbing Ruby's purse for her." Brianna opened the door and went to the small closet to grab Ruby's purse. Then they went to her classroom. She grabbed the kids' stuff and then her own.

Rafe stood in the doorway, watching, his eyes shifting back and forth as if he was expecting trouble. Once outside, she gave Ruby her purse and her kids what they needed before escorting them to their buses.

Brianna turned, and Rafe was right there. "How are you doing?" he asked as he walked her to her car.

"I'm okay. I was scared at first, but I'm good now."

"Did you see anything?"

"No. Just heard a big bang and then saw the smoke. The alarms went off a second later, and I got the kids out."

"Good job." Brianna pulled her keys from her purse and unlocked her vehicle. "I didn't know you were working today."

"I'm not. I was at the firehouse, talking with the Captain, when the alarm went off, and I came along." He stepped closer. "I was worried about you."

Brianna grinned. "I'm fine, especially when I realized there was no fire. I won't say I wasn't scared, because I was."

"God, I want to hold you, but…" He gestured to gear he wore. "Are we still good for tonight?"

"Yes. See you later."

Rafe leaned over and brushed his lips against hers. "I won't be so gentle later." He turned and walked away.

A very effective way to take her mind off the alarm this afternoon, she thought. Brianna's skin tingled her entire drive home.

* * * *

"No!"

Brianna's scream brought Rafe out of a sound sleep. He turned to see her head thrashing against the pillow, her face full of fear.

"Rafe…No!"

Her arms flew from side to side. Rafe sat up and captured her arms so she wouldn't hurt herself. "Brianna." No response. "Wake up, Brianna." This time, he put more force behind his words.

Her eyes popped open. Fear filled them, then she blinked. "Rafe?" He released her arms. Her hands went to his face. "You're here. You're okay." She was breathing heavy, as if she'd run a race.

"I'm fine, sweetheart." He shifted on the mattress and pulled her against him. "Bad dream?"

"The worst." A shudder went through her body.

"Want to tell me about it?" Brianna stayed silent. He began to worry.

She didn't answer right away, just kept hugging him tight. When she finally spoke, her voice was no more than a whisper. "There was a fire, and you rushed inside, only to be trapped. I watched the building burn with you inside it."

Oh, God. Her worst nightmare. Rafe tightened his hold on her. "It was a bad dream, probably brought on by today's events."

"Yes. But I can't shake it. Rafe, I don't want to lose you."

He wanted to reassure her she wouldn't lose him, but he didn't make promises he couldn't keep. While he did everything to be safe, something could happen, something no one could predict.

"I really want to promise you I'll be fine, but I can't. I follow the rules when I fight fires. I don't take chances." She snuggled closer, letting out a long, shuddering breath, then relaxed in his embrace. "You mean a lot to me, Brianna, and I don't want to lose you either."

She snuggled closer to him and kissed his chin. "Then we're on the same page."

"We are."

Brianna closed her eyes, but Rafe couldn't get back to sleep. Was he being selfish by keeping Brianna in his life? He didn't want her to have nightmares about fires or him being stuck in one. But this was his job. More than that. His vocation.

He wasn't sure how to resolve this issue or if there even was a resolution. Maybe on Monday, he'd talk to the chief about it.

* * * *

Brianna woke in Rafe's arms. Last night's nightmare flashed in her mind. She tilted her head to look at Rafe. His eyes were closed, his face relaxed.

He didn't dismiss her nightmare or her fear. The other thing was he didn't make a promise that he couldn't keep. Her parents used to tell her that another fire like the theirs couldn't happen again. That was a lie. There was no way to know for sure.

Rafe had held her and done his best to comfort her,

and that had gone a long way. She knew the nightmare had been triggered by what happened at school. It wasn't Rafe's fault.

He shifted in his sleep.

Brianna closed her eyes and soaked up his closeness, searching for a distraction. There was something she wanted to do tonight at the club, but she wasn't sure how he'd react.

* * * *

Sierra met Brianna in the ladies' room at Wicked Sanctuary.

"Are you sure about this?" Sierra asked.

"Yes." She'd been thinking about this and had talked with Sierra about how the fire cupping felt. Tonight, she was going to ask Rafe to demo it on her.

"Okay, here you go." Sierra handed her two nipple covers.

"Thank you." Brianna was still a little self-conscious about being nude, so this was a good compromise. Leaving off her sports bra, she put the nipple covers on. "Wow, you can't even tell I'm wearing anything."

"Yes, these are the best ones I've found. Tonight, when you take them off, if they start pulling on your skin too much, take a little baby power and sprinkle it. Also, make sure you wash them really well, and you can reuse them."

"You're the best, Sierra."

"Anything to help out my fellow subs." Sierra stared at her. "Does Rafe have any idea what you're going to ask him?"

"No. And I'm not sure if he'll accept my idea."

"Because of your fear of fire?"

"Yes. But, honestly, I watched him do the cupping

175

on you, and it looked heavenly and relaxing."

"It was very relaxing, and it really helped me feel better."

"You weren't feeling well?"

"I'm fine. Just tired. It energized me."

Brianna nodded, and together, they walked into the club. Brianna instantly spotted Rafe sitting at the bar with Max and chatting with Kaley behind the bar. Taking a big breath, Brianna walked over to them.

Max nudged Rafe, and he turned around. His eyes grew wide as he slid off the stool and stalked toward her. "Sierra," he acknowledged her, then his gaze locked on Brianna.

"See you later." Sierra left.

"Evening, Sir." Brianna tried to keep her tone even and soft. The smoldering look in Rafe's eyes increased her nervousness.

He swallowed. "You're…" Rafe shook his head. "You didn't need to do this for me." He waved his hand at her bare torso.

Brianna almost laughed. He hadn't noticed. "Are you paying attention, Sir?"

Rafe frowned.

"I'm not completely nude." She brushed her fingers over the nipple covers.

"You're wearing pasties?"

"They could be called that. I like nipple covers better, Sir."

"Why tonight?"

"Because…" She placed her hand on his arm, wanting to touch him as she asked. "I'd like you to do a fire cupping on me, Sir."

"You're not ready."

"But I am, Sir." She tightened her hold when he would have turned away. "I chatted with Sierra, and I'd really like to try it." She took a step closer. "I trust you, Sir. There is no open flame on my body or even nearby. Will you try it with me, please?"

Rafe closed his eyes and then opened them. "If I do this, there will only be two cups done. I won't leave them on more than two minutes, and if you get scared or feel they are too hot on your body, you are to tell me immediately."

"I can do that, Sir." Anticipation flowed through her veins.

"All right, let me ask Max if it's okay." Rafe took her hand in his and guided her over to where Max was sitting. "Max, Brianna would like to try fire cupping. Is it okay to do it tonight?"

Max glanced from Rafe to her, then nodded.

"This won't last long," Rafe said.

"That's okay. Whenever you want to do it," Max commented.

Rafe nodded. "First, I want you to hydrate." He helped her onto one of the stools and stood behind her, arms around her waist. "Water for Brianna, please, Kaley."

"Yes, Sir."

When Kaley brought back a bottle, Brianna opened it and began drinking. Sierra mentioned that Rafe had told her to be well hydrated before.

"We won't be able to do the cupping for at least another hour."

"Why is that, Sir?"

"Because we ate a late lunch at four, and it needs to be five hours after a meal before I do cupping. My rule.

Some will do between three and five; I like five."

"I can live with that, Sir."

"You don't have a choice," he whispered. "It also means no play tonight. I won't risk your health in any way."

"Okay, Sir." Brianna leaned back against Rafe as she drank her water, and they chatted with the others at the bar. He was going to do fire cupping on her. Her skin tingled. She felt like she was crawling out of her body, and at the same time, she wanted to run for the nearest exit, then she was back to wanting to demand Rafe start their fire play session.

And… Well, she hadn't told Rafe this, but she'd watched a couple of videos on fire cupping. It looked safe and everyone talked extensively about safety precautions. There was an ebb and flow at the bar she barely noticed until Rafe kissed the top of her head.

"I'm going to go get everything ready. Have Max or Noah bring you to the fire play room in fifteen minutes."

"Yes, Sir." She missed his warmth and steady presence after he left.

"Are you going to be okay doing this, Brianna?" Max asked.

"Yes, Sir. Sierra and I talked, plus watching Rafe do it made me want to try."

Max nodded. "I'll escort you over."

"Thank you, Sir." Brianna finished her water and glanced at Max. "I need to run to the ladies' room, Sir."

"Go."

Brianna walked out of the club and into the bathroom. She did have to go, but her heart wouldn't calm down. *Breathe.* In and out, she took deep breaths, and her momentary panic subsided.

Max was outside the bathroom when she came out. "I'm ready, Sir."

Max studied her for a moment, then nodded. Sierra walked out of the club and stood on one side of her. Max was on the other as they walked to the fire play room. Nerves caused Brianna's stomach to turn over in a good way. It was okay to be nervous. She'd never done this before.

She almost laughed out loud. There had been a lot of firsts with Rafe and Wicked Sanctuary. She looked forward—mostly—to this new one.

Rafe had everything laid out when they arrived. He took her hand and pulled her into the scene area. "Do you still want to do this?"

"Yes, Sir." She cupped his cheek. "I'll be fine, Sir. I want to try this."

Rafe nodded. There was still concern in his eyes, but he listened to her. "All right, let's get you onto the table." He helped her up.

Brianna folded her arms and laid her head on them, but she turned her face away from Rafe.

"I'm going to put a rolled-up towel over the back of your neck."

"Why, Sir?" He hadn't done that with Sierra.

"While there is no fire, I don't want to catch your hair with a cup. I shouldn't since I'm not doing it that high. Safety issue for me."

"Okay, Sir." She had a feeling Rafe was being extra careful with her. He placed the towel over her neck.

"Now, I'm going to rub oil on your back."

She jumped a little when the oil hit her skin, but Rafe massaging the oil into her skin over and over made her relax into his touch. She closed her eyes and let her mind just drift.

"Here we go," Rafe told her quietly.

The next sensation was something she couldn't really describe. There was warmth and the sensation of her skin being pulled tight once and then a second time. She immediately became calmer, more relaxed.

The pull on her skin wasn't unpleasant, just different. Then the suction was released. A rush of tranquility flowed over her as her skin settled. She laid there as Rafe poured more oil on her skin and rubbed it in. Then he covered her back with something.

"Are you okay?" he asked.

"Yes, Sir." While the scene itself had been short, her body seemed fully satisfied.

"Just lay there while I clean up."

Brianna didn't have a problem with that. She wasn't even sure she could stand. Sierra hadn't said anything about that, only that she'd been energized by the fire cupping. Now that Brianna could think, there was a strange buzzing through her body. It wasn't unpleasant, just unlike anything she'd experienced before.

"Brianna." Rafe's voice was soft. "Ready to get up?"

"You're done, already?"

"Yes."

Brianna lifted her head and straightened her arms, arching her back. Tingles spread out as the towel slipped down.

"I've got you." Rafe helped her swivel and sit with her legs over the table. With his hands at her waist, he lifted her up and into his arms. In the aftercare area, he sat with her in his lap, a blanket wrapped around her upper body. He handed her an open water bottle to drink from. "How do you feel?"

"Great, Sir. I didn't even hear you light the wand to do the fire part." That wasn't a bad thing either.

"You might feel some soreness tomorrow. The cupping can bring toxins out of your body. But you'll be with me, so you have nothing to worry about."

"I never do with you." She gazed up at him. "I loved what you did, Rafe."

His eyes grew wide.

"I know it's probably not the right time to say it, but…" He placed his fingers over her lips.

"It's the perfect time. I'm glad you wanted to try. We haven't known each other that long, and I didn't want to pressure you."

"You never pressure me." She realized that was true. "I'm so glad I met you, and you became my Dom."

"Same for me." He cradled her against his body. "Any pain?"

"Just some tingling, otherwise, no."

"Good. Just rest, and we'll go home in a bit and get a good night's sleep."

"Yes, Sir." Brianna closed her eyes, content to be in his arms.

* * * *

Rafe grinned from ear to ear when he walked into the firehouse on Monday. He and Brianna had spent a wonderful weekend together. She'd enjoyed the fire cupping, and he was in awe of her for taking that challenge on. He'd been worried at first that she was doing it to make him happy. But she'd convinced him she wasn't. Brianna was the most amazing woman he'd ever met.

Hell, he'd almost hit the floor when he thought she'd come into the club topless. Rafe didn't consider himself possessive, but found with Brianna, he didn't want her showing too much of her body in the club.

"Hey, Rafe," the captain called from his office.

"Yeah, Captain." Rafe leaned against the door frame.

"I'm going to need your expertise this morning." The captain pointed to the chair in front of his desk.

Rafe moved into the office and sat down. "What's going on?"

"Well, I think our little arsonist is back."

Rafe sat back in the chair. "What happened?"

The captain explained about two suspicious fires over the weekend, and he wanted another pair of eyes. They'd had so many fires lately that something wasn't adding up. At eight-thirty, the Captain and Rafe headed out to the first fire.

It was an old warehouse down by the water. While the Captain drove, Rafe questioned him about why he thought it was arson. The Captain gave his opinion, and once they got to the scene, they both made sure they were dressed properly before entering the warehouse.

Rafe stopped just inside the door and looked around for the point of origin. "It looks like it started in the back and moved forward."

"That was my deduction, as well. When we got here, the building was almost fully involved."

Rafe made his way slowly into the structure. The windows had heavy smoke deposits on them. Interesting. They shouldn't have been that damaged. When he made it to the next part of the warehouse, he stopped.

"It started here." The damage in this room was much worse. The windows had either cracked or been blown out, and there was a hint of something in the air. "There's a chemical smell." Rafe studied the floor. "And the burn pattern is wrong."

"That's what I thought. Shall we head over to the other one?"

"Yes. I can come back to this one with more equipment and take samples." Rafe ran his hand over his face. He had a feeling he knew what he'd find, and it would match some of the other investigations.

The next one was an empty store front in town. By the grace of God, the fire hadn't spread to any of the other stores. This one had the same pattern. "Damn, this isn't looking good," Rafe said.

"That's why I wanted your opinion."

"I hate to say we have a serial arsonist, but we've had too many fires." Rafe shook his head.

"I agree. I didn't want to jump to conclusions. At first, I thought maybe it was kids playing around, but now I'm not so sure."

"Let me grab some equipment and see what else I can determine, but I'd let the higher ups know what we've found."

"On it." They walked back to the truck.

Once back at the firehouse, Rafe grabbed his arson equipment, loaded it into the small truck that belonged to the fire department, then drove back out to the first scene. He really hoped this was kids, but he had a feeling it wasn't.

Rafe took his time at each scene, including talking with the neighbors of the empty store and near the warehouse to find out if anyone had seen or heard anything. He also stopped by the police station and picked up the preliminary police reports.

After dropping off his samples at the lab, he went back to the firehouse and set up in the conference room.

He pulled all the reports of the fires over the last three months to see if he could find a pattern. It was going to be a long week.

At least he could look forward to seeing Brianna. When he worked until six, she had him come by her place, and they ate dinner together. She was a much better cook than she liked to believe. He didn't spend the night—much as he wanted to—but it didn't stop him from kissing or touching her.

He rubbed his forehead as he put another file on the not-arson pile. Something wasn't adding up here, and he was determined to figure out what it was.

Chapter 14

Brianna walked around her classroom on Thursday afternoon, watching the kids draw. She was so glad tomorrow was Friday. She liked her job, but she couldn't wait to spend more time with Rafe.

Maybe it was time to admit that she'd fallen in love with him. The thought should have surprised her, but it didn't. Rafe was a special man, and she didn't want to let him go. She had no idea if he felt the same about her.

In and out of the club, they enjoyed each other, be it a quiet dinner together, cuddling on the sofa and watching a movie, and in the bedroom with or without kink. For once in her life, she felt settled and not like she was looking for something she couldn't find.

"That's pretty," she commented to Penny, who had drawn a butterfly. Brianna turned, and there was a huge bang. She jumped as some of the kids screamed. Fighting to remain calm, to not give in to her own panic, she motioned for the kids to quiet. "Settle down," she said firmly.

The sound had come from the hallway. Brianna moved to the door of her classroom. She saw smoke. Fire! Again? Her heart pounded, and her palms grew moist. Forcing air into her lungs, she turned back to her students.

"We're leaving the classroom. There is possible a

fire; let's line up." She clapped her hands. The kids' eyes grew wide, but they lined up and held hands. "Everyone, follow Jasper once we get into the hallway."

"Yes, Miss Brianna."

Brianna eased the door open to lots of dense smoke, and she could see red haze to her left. This wasn't like the last time. "Jasper, go to the right and out the back door. Assemble in our spot by the playground. And walk, do not run."

"Yes, Miss Brianna. This way, everyone." Jasper's calm voice helped Brianna.

Was the fire advancing? She couldn't tell. There was too much smoke. The last of her kids left the classroom, and Brianna followed them out. Her breath came in short pants as she focused on them and told herself over and over not to look back.

Once outside, the kids broke away and ran for their meeting place. "No running," she yelled, but could she blame them? Twice in as many weeks now, this had happened. Who was doing this?

Other classes were exiting. Brianna focused on her kids. Many were coughing. She caught up with them and started her head count.

There was one missing. Her heart leaped into her throat. She'd counted as they left the classroom. All fifteen had been in line, so who was missing? Brianna counted again and said each child's name in her head.

"Where's Andy?"

"He ran back in for his hamster," Suzie said.

"Jasper, lead everyone over to Miss Ruby." And to the other children, "Go with Jasper."

"Yes, Miss Brianna."

Brianna turned on her heels and ran back to the

building. The smoke was thicker now. Her heart threatened to burst from her chest. Oh. My. God. There were flames very near her classroom door. Fighting panic, she raced ahead.

"Andy," she yelled as she darted into her classroom and slammed the door.

"Miss Brianna," Andy called. He was curled up in the back corner of the room, coughing.

Moving quickly, she gathered him into her arms.

"I'm sorry, but I couldn't let my hamster get burned." His voice was raspy.

"I understand." She glanced at the door. Flames now licked the outside of it. She concentrated on the way the fire moved. Now what? Were those sirens? Fire department? God, she hoped so, because she was starting to panic.

Think, Brianna. She glanced around her room. The window. She'd left it open. Was it big enough? Well, they were about to find out.

* * * *

Rafe jumped into the fire truck with the others as they took off. His gut churned. The elementary school was on fire. Brianna was his first thought. They were the closest to the school, but the chief had already called in two other houses to be on the safe side.

The truck pulled into the parking lot, and Rafe leaped out as it stopped. Flames shot from the roof of the school. Fighting his urge to go find Brianna, he started pulling the hoses from the truck and hooking them up, his eyes darting everywhere.

Tim grabbed the hose. "Go find her."

Rafe looked at the chief, who nodded. He glanced around, looking again for Brianna, but he couldn't see her. Then he saw her class standing with another teacher. "Do you know where Brianna is?" he asked.

"She went back inside to get Andy," one of the kids said.

His heart froze. She ran back into the fire. No… She was afraid. Looking around, he found the principal and ran over to her. "Is there anyone else missing?"

"Just Brianna and Andy. I can't believe she went back into the school."

Rafe didn't hesitate; he ran back to the truck. "Chief, we have a teacher and student inside the school." He grabbed another hose and headed for Brianna's classroom.

"Rafe," the chief yelled his name and put a hand on his arm. "We'll take care it."

"But…"

"Rules. You're involved." The chief yelled at the others. "Where is her classroom?"

Rafe told them and watched as others went into the school to fight the fire and find his Brianna. Yes, she was his. He was in love with her and couldn't see his life without her.

Why did that realization come to him now? He glanced at the kids. Many were crying and upset, especially those in Brianna's class. He couldn't do anything, so he walked up to the class and began comforting the kids.

He told them Brianna and Andy would be all right. He had to believe that. His fellow firefighters were good. Hopefully Brianna and Andy hadn't been overcome by smoke. That was sometimes more deadly than fire.

There were shouts, and he glanced over at the doorway to see a group of firefighters backing out. What the hell? He noticed the roof was coming down. Damn. They needed to find Brianna now.

A hand settled on his shoulder, and Rafe jumped, turning to see the other teacher. "I'm Ruby, Brianna's friend. Parents are starting to arrive, so I need to take the kids to the other side of the parking lot. The parents are frantic."

"I bet." He helped her usher the kids around the grass to the pick-up zone as parents began pouring into the area. Several of Brianna's kids didn't want to leave.

"We'll find Brianna and Andy. They'll be fine." Rafe assured everyone until their parents arrived.

He had no idea how he was going to keep that promise. Rafe pictured her classroom in his mind. She was mid-way down the hall, two exits at each end of the hallway, and…windows. To hell with standing back. He needed to save his woman. Rafe ran around the side of the building.

Brianna's shout made his heart race. That's when he saw a man dressed in a dark hoodie and jeans, holding something in his hand. It was then he realized Brianna and Andy were standing on the ground, outside the burning school, about ten feet from the guy.

She was safe. Relief hit him along with another shot of adrenaline. Rafe shouted at the guy, who dropped what he was holding and ran. Rafe went after him. It wasn't much of a race even with the gear he wore. Rafe caught up with him and tackled him to the ground. The man tried to buck him off, but Rafe knew how to hold him down.

"We've got it, Rafe."

Rafe turned his head to see Logan and two other officers standing there. He eased up and let Logan take over, then he turned. Where was Brianna? His gaze roamed the area, and he saw her with a team of paramedics.

"I'm okay, really," Brianna said to the paramedics.

"You should keep the oxygen on, ma'am."

"I don't need it." She pushed the man's arm away and glanced over at the little boy sitting next to her. "How are you doing, Andy?"

"I'm good, Miss Brianna." A little pink nose peeked out from the boy's shirt. "So is Mr. Hammy."

"Good." She glanced up and met Rafe's gaze. "Stay right here." Brianna stood and walked toward him.

Rafe's long strides met her before she got more than a few feet from the paramedics. "You should listen to the paramedics," he said. Would his heart ever calm down?

"As I told them. I'm fine." Just then, there was a shout, and a blonde woman raced toward the paramedics. "That's Andy's mom. Be right back."

He kept his gaze on her as she talked with the mother and then the father when he arrived. Andy sat there as his parents alternately scolded him, then hugged him and told him he was a good kid. The mother hugged Brianna before she took Andy's hand and dad took Mr. Hammy.

"Wait," Andy called out and pulled away from his mother. "Thank you for saving me, Miss Brianna." The little boy hugged her tight, released her, and joined his parents.

Rafe slipped his arms around her waist and pulled her against him. "Mr. Hammy?"

"The hamster. Andy's show and tell today. He went back in to get him."

"And you went in after Andy." The pieces were starting to come together.

"What else could I do? He's one of my kids."

Rafe sighed and released her as the principal walked up to them along with the chief.

"Fire is out," the chief said.

"Thank goodness," Brianna said with a shiver.

"Andy is no worse for wear. How are you, Brianna?" the principal asked.

"I'm fine. I'm guess there will be no school for a while." She glanced back at the smoldering ruins of the school.

"I'll start working with the school board and find room for our students, but it will be probably a week or more before we can find a places, virtual doesn't do well for us. Go home, and I'll be in contact." The principal walked away.

"I have no idea how I'm going to get home," Brianna said.

"Don't you have your car here?" the chief asked.

"Yes, but my keys and stuff are still in my classroom, as I'm sure it is with all the teachers."

"Where are your belongings located?" Rafe asked.

"Bottom right drawer." She frowned at him.

"Be right back."

"Rafe." She called his name, but he kept going. He rounded the building and found her classroom from the outside and noticed the open window. So that's how she got out. It would be tight, but he maneuvered through the window, found her bag, and climbed back out.

Brianna was talking to the captain until the captain gestured over her shoulder. She turned to glare at him when he returned with her bag.

"I think I'll let Rafe drive you home. Rafe, take care of her." The chief walked away.

Brianna yanked her purse from his hold. "Of all the

stupid things to do, go back into a building that's all but collapsed from fire damage." She threw her hands up, the strap of her purse snapping. "Ugh." She held it way from her. "This thing smells horrible."

Rafe started laughing. He didn't know what else to do, and honestly, the sheer relief of her arguing with him was like a pressure valve going off. He pulled her into his arms and hugged her tight.

She returned the hug just as tight. "I don't know what I'd do without out you, Rafe."

"I'm here, sweetheart. Forever and always."

Rafe placed his hand on her elbow. "What about the other teachers?" she asked, glancing around and seeing the mingling.

"The chief will clear the school and help them get their belongings."

"Okay. Let me go say good bye."

As much as he wanted to whisk Brianna away, he didn't. She talked with a couple of the teachers, then hugged Ruby, before making her way back to him. They walked to her car, and she dug her keys out of her purse.

"I'll drive," he said, and held out his hand.

She looked him up and down. "In that?"

Rafe glanced down. He was still in his turn-outs. "Easy fix." He undid the protective gear and watched Brianna's mouth drop open as he stripped out if it.

"You wear other clothes underneath."

"Yes. Did you think I didn't?"

"I didn't know what to expect."

Rafe laughed. "Keys."

She dropped them in his palm after unlocking the doors. Rafe deposited his turn-outs in the back seat before getting in the driver's side. Within fifteen minutes, they were at his home. Thank goodness, too, because Brianna kept clearing her throat.

"Your turn-outs smell as bad as my purse."

"I'll put them both in the garage to air out."

Brianna looked around. "I thought you were taking me home."

"I am." He parked her car in the driveway, then helped her out of the vehicle and into the house. In his mind and heart, this was her home now. They belonged together. Once in the family room, he gathered her into his arms and sat on the sofa with her in his lap.

Rafe took a deep breath. "I was so scared for you." He wasn't going to hide his emotions.

"I'm sorry." She laid her head on his shoulder and relaxed in his embrace. "I couldn't leave Andy in there."

"I know you talked with the chief as the paramedics checked you out. What did you tell him?"

"I didn't know much. Mainly, I told him about seeing the guy you were chasing and hearing a loud bang before the fire started."

"Damn arsonist," he muttered.

"Is that who he is?"

"I can't say for sure, but it's very suspicious. The chief will keep everyone out until we can investigate."

"But you said he'd get the others' belongings?"

He kissed her forehead. "He will, but they'll do it through the windows if need be. Everyone will be safe."

"Why not just walk in and get it?"

"In order to prove arson, we need to preserve the scene until the investigation is done."

"Why the school?"

"I can't explain that. I don't know why anyone would want to hurt kids. Do you know of any threats against the school?" It could have been a disgruntled parent, but it wasn't usual to see an arsonist escalate.

"Not that I know of. The principal would know for sure." She cuddled closer to him.

"What were you thinking? You're afraid of flames."

"I wasn't thinking. Well, that's not true." Her smile was small. "You've taught me how, and with the fire cupping, you showed me I don't need to be afraid. I listened and paid attention."

"But still." He tightened his arms around her. "Smoke inhalation kills faster than fire."

"As you've told me before, and I was as careful as I could be. Trust me, I wasn't about to let Andy or myself die. I have too much to live for." She lifted her arm, and her palm cupped his cheek. "I love you."

A jolt shot through his body. "You…love me?" Was he hearing her correctly?

"Yes." She brushed her lips over his. "I love you."

"I never expected…" He paused to catch his breath. "I love you too. When I heard you ran back into the fire, I was out of my mind with worry."

"Oh, honey. Don't get me wrong. I was scared to death. But during our talks, you talked to me about how fire burns, and I knew what to look for. Unfortunately, it spread before Andy and I could get back out the door. So we climbed out the window."

"You're perfect." He captured her lips with his. "I love you so much. I should have told you before now."

"We aren't on a timetable, and we've only been together a few months. I didn't expect it to happen, but today, standing in my classroom with Andy and the fire trying to break in, I knew I couldn't leave you. You are a sweet, lovable gentleman and the perfect Dom for me."

Damn, this woman could unman him with simple words. "Enough talk." He put one arm under her legs and the other across her back as he stood. "Time for us." He strode to his bedroom.

Chapter 15

Rafe woke with Brianna in his arms. After they showered last night, they made love, called for pizza, and made love again. Today was a new start for both of them. His cell buzzed, and he grabbed it. "Just a second," he said. He eased Brianna from his arms, climbed out of bed, and made his way into the kitchen.

"What's up, boss?"

"I know it's your day off, but would you come by the school? I want to you to go over the scene. The principal is anxious to get a clean-up crew in here."

"Sure. Can you give me an hour?" It was eight now.

"Meet me there at ten."

The line went dead. Rafe put on coffee and looked through his fridge. Breakfast would need to be quick this morning.

"Good morning," a sleepy Brianna said from behind him.

He turned to see her in his robe, hair mussed, looking absolutely delicious. "Morning." He pulled her in for a kiss, but she held up her hand.

"Morning breath."

"Who cares." He gave her a kiss. When he lifted his head, she sighed.

"Who was on the phone?"

"My boss. I need to meet him at the school at ten."

"Okay, let me get cleaned up and dressed."

"You don't have to go with me." He didn't want her to relive any element of the fire.

"I want to."

"You can't go inside. It's an active scene."

"I'm okay with that, but I want to be there." She walked out of the room. "Don't worry about breakfast; coffee and toast is fine for me," she yelled.

Rafe shook his head.

* * * *

"It doesn't look too bad from the outside," Brianna said as they pulled up to the school.

"It's the inside that's the issue. Plus, we need to check out the building to make sure it's structurally safe."

Brianna climbed out of Rafe's SUV, and together they walked up to the chief and the principal.

"I wasn't expecting you, Brianna," the principal said.

"I thought you could use some support while Rafe and the Chief do their job." That was one of the reasons. The other: she needed to see if she'd really confronted her fear.

"I thank you for that. While they inspect the school, let's talk over by my vehicle. I have some ideas I'd like to run past you on what we can do until our school is rebuilt."

Brianna looked at Rafe, who nodded.

For the next hour, Brianna and the principal went over plans of where each class would be housed, and how they could help their students recover from the fire. Parents were already asking what was going to happen.

"Thanks. I think we've got a good plan in place," the principal said.

"I'm glad I could help. Will we start classes on

Monday?" It made sense to get the kids back to a normal routine.

"I think we'll do an assembly on Monday and invite the parents. I've already talked with the high school; we can use their auditorium."

"That would be good. Get the parents involved." It was going to take a lot of work, classroom wise. All their stuff was in their school classrooms and who knew in what condition.

"The town council is already working to get new supplies for the classes."

"Maybe we can contact some of the local businesses in town and see if we can get some donations." It would help with the financial strain this fire was going to cause. The sound of tires made them both turn.

Brianna's eyes widened when Sierra, Crystal, Tessa, and Ellie climbed out of the big black SUV. "Principal Meyers, these are my friends." Brianna introduced them. "What are you doing here?" she asked them.

Sierra smiled. "We wanted to come and tell you and the principal, of course, that Wicked Sanctuary is chipping in. We've already ordered as many supplies as we could think of for the kids."

"Excuse me?" The principal looked shocked.

Tessa stepped forward. "I'm a librarian and have worked with a couple of your teachers. I have a pretty good idea what's needed. We already have books, art supplies, boards, and other things for the students, and just need to know where it can all be stored until the classes are settled."

Crystal stepped forward. "And you have labor—us— to help the teachers set up their classrooms and get things in order so the kids don't feel out of place."

"I also have supplies that we can use to decorate the classroom, plus we'd like to host a party for each classroom to welcome the kids."

"Oh my goodness." The principal put her hand over her heart. "This is very unexpected."

Brianna's heart swelled.

"We don't want the kids to suffer. We all agreed, along with our significant others," Sierra said.

"I don't know what to say." Principal Meyers had tears in her eyes.

"I don't either," Brianna admitted. This was so unexpected.

"You don't have to say anything. All we need is to know when and where to show up," Crystal commented.

"How about I call you with the information this weekend," Brianna offered. Everything they'd offered was a bit overwhelming.

"Perfect." Sierra swept Brianna into a hug. "Hopefully, we'll see you tonight."

Brianna nodded, staring after her friends as they left. She was so lucky.

"I didn't expect such generosity," Principal Meyers said. "I was never sure about the club, but I can see they're a positive part of our community."

"You know about Wicked Sanctuary?" Why was Brianna so surprised at that?

"After the town council's support, let's see, about two years ago, I don't think there's anyone in town who doesn't know. I've always said to each their own. And that goes for you, too, young lady." The principal turned her head. "And here comes your young man."

Brianna turned to see Rafe walking toward them complete in his turn-outs, gloves, and respirator. Damn if he didn't look hot. Almost too hot.

"Well?" the principal asked.

"We're done. There is some instability, but I can escort your teachers in to gather what supplies they can salvage. It will be one at a time. The sprinklers, plus our efforts to put out the fire, did a lot of damage," the captain said.

"Not unexpected. I'll let the town council know and see when they can get someone out here to start cleaning this mess up. I have a feeling they'll need to tear the building down and rebuild." Principal Meyers shook her head. "Thank you for all your help." She went to shake their hands. Both men pulled off their gloves.

"I'll be in touch," the captain said as the principal walked to her car, then he looked at Rafe. "We'll go over your report on Monday. Have a good weekend." With that, the chief left.

Rafe stripped out of his turn-outs and put them in the trunk.

"Was it arson?" Brianna asked.

"Yes." He rubbed his forehead. "It's going to be a while before the school will be ready for students."

"I get that," she broke off as a truck pulled up. Two men got out. She knew them; they were from the club.

"Rafe, Brianna," one said.

"Zeke, Gabriel, what can we do for you?" Rafe asked.

Yes, those were their names.

"I was hoping," Gabriel said, "that Brianna can put us in touch with whomever we need to so we can discuss fixing the school."

"Fixing the school?" Briana asked unsure what Gabriel was talking about.

"I'm Riggs Construction, and Gabriel is my architect. We want to donate our time and materials to getting the school fixed up and the kids back where they belong."

Brianna was unable to stop the tears filling her eyes. So much generosity. The Wicked Sanctuary family was gathering around her and putting the kids first. She never expected this.

"We're also getting lots of help," Gabriel added.

"Like what?" Brianna could fathom this.

"Dani is going to do landscaping for the school, and I believe Sierra and few of the others told you about the supplies," Zeke said.

"Yes, they left a little bit ago." Brianna took Rafe's hand in hers.

"Great. Lara is going to provide food for any parties you need. Most of the guys will be muscle to help moving anything," Gabriel said.

"So many."

"Welcome to the Wicked Sanctuary family," Rafe said, grinning.

EPILOGUE

Rafe wrapped his arms around Brianna as they stood in the club three months later. Things had moved rather quickly since the fire at the school. Once permission was granted, the old school was torn down and the new one built.

Zeke, Gabriel, and their construction team had the new school built in no time. It helped that Zeke's fiancée, Allyson, worked at the city planning and urban development office. She was able to get the permits and inspections done in record time.

The Wicked Sanctuary family had stepped up to the plate, from rebuilding the school to getting supplies the teachers needed, helping the teachers set up in their temporary space, and then decorating their new classrooms.

The principal was so overwhelmed with it all. She thanked everyone personally when they had a small party at the school for the teachers. An unknown in the plans was that a bigger place for the students to eat and more playground equipment had been added.

"I've been meaning to ask about the kid you caught running away from the school." They'd talked about it, but she'd gotten caught up with her students and now moving back into the new school.

"I forgot to tell you about the call I got today. You know that I was able to connect him to several other fires."

"Yes."

"Apparently, today, he confessed that he'd set them all. He's over eighteen, so he'll be tried as an adult."

"But why the school?" She never understood that.

"His little brother goes there and was bullied by a couple of other kids. He admitted the other places were trial runs."

Brianna frowned. "We don't tolerate bullying in any way, shape, or form."

"It was only once. It wasn't until the big brother confronted his little brother, that the kid broke down and told the big brother what happened."

"Goodness."

"Yeah." Rafe leaned over and kissed her temple. "He's got a long road ahead of him, but his parents have already told the court they'll do whatever is needed to help both sons."

"That's good." She relaxed into his embrace.

"Happy?" Rafe asked, his arms tightening around Brianna.

"Very. I do have one question for you."

"Yes."

"I want to try fire wands."

"We've talked about his." Rafe turned her in his arms.

"I know. But I really want to try. I'm not afraid of fire with you, Rafe. I've learned so much about it; I'm not as bothered by it as I was."

"This is different."

"Is it? I've been able to sit with you around the fire pit with a live fire. I know you won't hurt me or cause any harm. I trust you."

Rafe swallowed. "Let me think about it."

"That's all I ask. Besides, I love you."

"I love you too."

"Good, because I'm not letting you get away from me, Sir."

"There's no other person I want to be with." Rafe kissed her. Maybe, in another few months, he'd be ready to do the fire wands with her. But for right now, he was going to keep her safe in his arms.

* * * *

Across the room, Max held Sierra in his arms as they looked over their friends at Wicked Sanctuary.

"Our lives have changed so much in the last few years," Max said.

"Yes, they have." Sierra tilted her head back. "I want to do a big Christmas party for our intimate Wicked Sanctuary family."

"Is it going to be like that Halloween party last year?" He was still trying to get over what the women had done.

"Same group with a few added, and our Wicked Sanctuary family, because that's what we are."

"Anything you want, my sweet."

"Thank you." Sierra turned and hugged him.

Max would never get tired of Sierra, and he would probably never deny her anything. "Please don't go crazy decorating. Halloween almost killed me."

"I promise it won't be crazy. It's going to be a celebration."

The glint of mischief in Sierra's eyes told him she was planning something. "Are you feeling okay? You've been really tired lately."

"I'm good."

There was that twinkle again. Max knew he was in deep, deep trouble with her. And there was no other place he'd rather be.

ABOUT THE AUTHOR

Marie Tuhart lives in the beautiful Pacific Northwest with her two dogs, Tommy and Trina. Marie brings to life contemporary approachable alpha heroes and the spunky women who take them to task. Her high-heat, emotional books, many with BDSM elements, inviting the reader to slid the silky scarves between their fingers, fell the kiss of a flogger on their flesh in breathless anticipation of what or who will come next. Embrace the temptation and enjoy a happily ever after that's always about the heroine.

And for up-to-date information about releases, please consider joining Marie's mailing list.

* * * *

Thank you for reading *Too Hot,* the final book in the Wicked Sanctuary series. If you enjoyed this book, please consider leaving a review on Goodreads, or your favorite retailer. It is greatly appreciated. For new release information and news about Marie Tuhart, please join her newsletter.

There will be a Wicked Sanctuary Christmas, a novella, showing you the lives of the main characters in the series. This is a special book for readers to have. You will receive a free copy if you join my newsletter when the book releases at the end of September.

In August, I will be releasing Embracing Desire. Follow reunited lovers in a why choose contemporary spicy book with a quirky grandmother and a small town that looks out for each other. Pre order here:

https://books2read.com/EmbracingDesire

OTHER BOOKS BY MARIE TUHART

Claimed by the Sheikh
Billionaire's Cowboy's Conquest
More of You (Club Crave)
Reflections of you (Club Crave)
Bound to Love You (Club Crave)
Hot for You (Club Crave)
Tempt (Wicked Sanctuary Series)
Entice (Wicked Sanctuary Series)
Seduce (Wicked Sanctuary Series)
Ravish (Wicked Sanctuary Series)
Possess (Wicked Sanctuary Series)
Tantalize (Wicked Sanctuary Series)
Edged (Wicked Sanctuary Series)
Unmasked (Wicked Sanctuary Series)
Too Hot (Wicked Sanctuary Series)

Wicked Sanctuary Novellas:
Untamed
Power Play
Claiming Rose

9 781954 847118